A LETTER FROM JULIETTE CARLTON

Greensville, NC

September

I could tell you a story about how my uncle Grey Alexander left me Magnolia Hall because I was his favorite niece. About how on the day he died I found out he made sure I, Juliette Carlton, a forty-year-old, three-time divorced blackjack dealer, his beloved niece and misplaced Southern belle, inherited all he had, including the memories of a loving Southern family.

But none of it would be true.

And before all this happened, I believed money would make my life better, different, worth living. What I didn't know was that no amount of money could help me. It took something so strange to make me see what's really important.

Mary Schramski

Mary Schramski began writing when she was about ten. The first story she wrote took place at a junior high school. Her mother told her it was good, so she immediately threw it away. She read F. Scott Fitzgerald at eleven, fell in love with storytelling and decided to teach English. She holds a Ph.D in creative writing and enjoys teaching and encouraging other writers. She lives in Nevada with her husband, and her daughter who lives close by. Visit Mary's Web site at www.maryschramski.com.

what to KEEP

MARY SCHRAMSKI

WHAT TO KEEP

copyright © 2005 Mary L. Schramski

i s b n 0 3 7 3 8 8 0 5 8 8

This edition published by arrangement with Harlequin Books S.A.

TheNextNovel.com

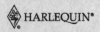 HARLEQUIN®

PRINTED IN U.S.A.

From the Author

Dear Reader,

You and I have a connection. I'm a reader, too. When I hold a book in my hands, an excitement begins because, with just the turn of the page, the possibilities are endless. And I believe novels polish hearts and souls to a lovely brilliance.

I wrote *What To Keep* because I want you to experience a Southern town and live in an old Southern mansion. I want you to become acquainted with a woman who inherits her family's home and all the memories that go along with it. Most of all, I want you to breathe Southern air, taste a bit of Southern food and hear the singsong cadence of a Southern accent.

Come on, take my hand, let's go together.

Mary

www.maryschramski.com

To my editor, Gail Chasan, who has been my guide
and the ultimate professional.

PROLOGUE

Greensville, NC
September 2000

I could tell you a story about how my uncle Grey Alexander left me Magnolia Hall because I was his favorite niece. Then you might think I visited him every summer to attend reunions, and our family was close and very loving. That's when I'd explain that Uncle Grey always sent me beautiful birthday cards, telephoned me on Christmas morning to wish me a happy, peaceful holiday. And at the end of our conversation he'd go on and on about how he wished I were home instead of in dusty Las Vegas.

I'd also tell you on the day he died I found out he made sure I, Juliette Carlton, a forty-year-old, three-times-divorced blackjack dealer, his beloved niece and misplaced Southern belle, inherited all he had, including the memories of a loving Southern family.

But none of it would be true.

Someone once told me the reason people lie is because it sounds better. They were right. And life, as my mother used to remind me over and over, is raw and ugly. Part of that is true. Life is raw and ugly if a person makes it that way. Maybe that's why my mother lied so much.

I've decided not to fabricate anything, especially to myself. At one time I was big on that. I'd tell myself I was happy when I wasn't, tell myself a man cared when he didn't.

So the truth is I inherited an old Southern house from a man who just happened to be my uncle. I barely had a few faded memories of him. I became the owner of his house because I'm the only family member left. And that one little mistake of Grey Alexander not making a will changed my life forever. Because before all this happened I believed money would make my life better, different, worth living. What I didn't know was that no amount of money could help me. It took something so strange, like inheriting an old Southern mansion that shouldn't have belonged to me, to make me see what's really important.

CHAPTER 1

Las Vegas, NV
June 2000

Barbara, the only other female blackjack dealer on day shift, just tapped me on the shoulder for my break. I've been dealing blackjack to two deadbeat guys for the past forty minutes. Dealers deal for forty minutes, then break for twenty, over and over until their eight-hour shifts are finished, just like in a factory—in this case, a big, smoky money machine.

I clap my hands to show I'm not stealing chips, and I'm halfway down the middle of the pit when the pit boss motions me over to the center podium.

"Message for you," Joe says. He adds, "Casino policy says no personal phone calls." Even so, he hands me the yellow Post-it note he's holding between his thumb and forefinger. Joe, as always, is wearing plenty of gold jewelry. And I just know his navy suit must have cost him at least a thousand. Joe makes two thousand a month before taxes watching people deal cards. Most pit bosses try to pretend they own the casino, probably just to make their lives bearable.

"Thanks," I force myself to say. I've worked at the Golden Nugget for three years. Joe has only been here six months, and he's been on my ass since the first day he walked into the pit. He's asked me to go out and have a drink but of course he doesn't talk about his wife when he suggests we walk across the street to the Horseshoe after work. He's just trying to get laid. Casino bosses think they have a right to the help, but even if I found him attractive, I'm totally through with men, especially men like Joe who pretend they have more than they do, or that they're single, or both.

I fold the Post-it note in half, smile and walk back to the break room. A moment later I unfold the yellow square. Joe printed "Ron Tanner," a name I don't recognize. And now I'm thinking Bill, my ex, might be in a jam. And this scares me, how easily he can pop into my mind. I've been working extra hard to forget. Guess I've got to try harder.

I walk over to the table by the pay phone, pick up the phone book and check the area code. Whoever Ron Tanner is, he's calling from the western half of North Carolina. And he probably doesn't have anything to do with Bill. That man, I am sure, has never been east of the Arizona border.

However, my father was born and buried in North Carolina, and he, my mother and I lived there for a brief time. I have one uncle who lives there, but we haven't seen each other or spoken in thirty-five years. I ball up the tiny piece of paper and walk to the trash. Before I can pitch it, my curiosity gets the best of me. A moment later I dial the number using the last bit of credit on my phone card.

The voice on the other end announces law offices. I tell myself to hang up. With Bill, I found out law offices can only mean trouble with a capital pain in the ass, but instead I identify myself and ask to speak to Ron Tanner.

A minute later, in a strong Southern accent, Ron Tanner announces that he's acting as the court-appointed executor for Grey Alexander's estate. I hear him take a deep breath then, at a quick pace, he explains he's sorry to have to tell me, but my uncle passed away three weeks ago, and I have inherited his estate because I'm his only living relative.

"Are you all right?" he asks.

"Yes. What happened to my uncle?" I ask, confused.

"He had cancer. From what I understand he fought it for quite a while. I'm very sorry."

"Thank you."

There's a long silence while my mind tries to wrap around what I've just been told.

"I'm sure you have a few questions," Ron says.

A little sound like "oh" bounces out of my mouth.

"No?"

"Sorry. What exactly do you mean by *estate*?"

"It consists of your uncle's house and his belongings, which aren't much."

My *uncle*. I hadn't thought of him in years, and now all of a sudden I have his house.

"Are you okay?" he asks, his smooth, deep accent getting deeper.

"Yeah, I'm okay, just surprised." I shake my head—feel dizzy. When was the last time I saw my uncle? Then I remember. My dad, mother and I were driving away from my uncle's house. Grey Alexander, a tall man with blond hair, in a navy jacket and cream pants, was standing on the front porch of his large house, his arms crossed, staring at our car. I waved a five-year-old goodbye—he never lifted his hand.

"I certainly had difficulty locating you," Ron Tanner breaks in. "Do you know your phone's disconnected?"

Did I know? I've been without a phone for a month, hoofing it down to the 7-Eleven on Sunset and Green Valley Parkway to make calls in an attempt to straighten out the mess Bill left me in. But I don't tell Ron Tanner this. He probably doesn't want to hear my sad story.

"What exactly is in Grey Alexander's estate?" I ask, and then remember I've already asked this.

"A house. A car. Not much else."

"What's the house like?" I wonder if it is the same one, the one I stared at through the back window of our family car, the same one where I ran down the hallway to a roomy kitchen.

Ron explains it's very old and pretty run-down.

"How do I sell it?" I ask, thinking about the extra money I so desperately need.

"You might consider coming back to Greensville. The house has to be inspected. Then you could talk to a Realtor."

I think about how Joe hates me 'cause I won't go out with him; he would never let me off, even for a few days.

"I can't. I have to work. No vacation left. Can I get in touch with a Realtor from here? Have her take care of the inspection?"

"You can," Ron says. "I can get you a few names."

Moments later, still dazed and wondering if this is all a big joke, I cradle the phone and lean against the wall. Leanne, the break-room waitress, walks up to me, glances at her watch and asks if I want anything to eat. I look up.

"Are you okay?"

I shake my head, blurt out I've just inherited a house in North Carolina.

"You're lying!"

"No, it's true, or at least I think it is. I just spoke with the attorney."

"I'm so sorry about your loss."

"I really didn't know the person."

Leanne pats my shoulder then steps back a little. "Well, now there's no excuse not to get out of this hellhole."

My mother, when I'd talked about moving away from Vegas, always placed her hand on her chest, right in the middle and whispered how alone she was in the world, how she needed me. Which now, years later, I know was total bullshit. But her drama gave me a good excuse for not moving—this glittering desert town sucks people into its dreams.

Leanne's brown eyes grow larger. "When are you going to see your house?"

I shake my head. "I'm not. I've got to work, and I don't have any extra money."

She stuffs her hands in her pockets and looks hard at me. "Are you kidding? Someone loves you enough to leave you a house, all their things, and you aren't going to go and look at them? You're crazy."

I think about telling her that my getting the house doesn't have anything to do with love, but what's the point? Grey Alexander didn't leave me his house; some probate judge flung it to me because I'm from a small family.

"I don't have the money to go," I say again, and this is so true. Bill left me in debt, took almost everything good we owned. "Besides, Joe isn't going to let me off for a week. The lawyer said he'd give me the name of a Realtor who would handle everything."

Leanne sighs. "What's a Supersaver cost? I never saw a house sell for anything without the owner being there. We sold our house up in Salt Lake after we moved down here and got screwed. You'd better get back there and take care of business."

I stand, wish I hadn't told her about the call. "I'd better get back to the pit before I get the ax."

Leanne shakes her head, clucks her tongue and heads toward the kitchen.

I slip my time card in the clock, and the deep thunk clocks me out at 8:01 p.m. The Golden Nugget time office pulses with boredom, greasy concrete floors, and bright fluorescent lighting that shows too much reality. Up front the casino, restaurant, and lounge are all gold, red and satin under soft lighting. Back here, this is the truth. The timekeeper nods and I walk down the stairs into the parking lot. Furnacelike air engulfs me. Eight o'clock at night and it is still eighty-five degrees. For the next three months the desert heat will cook everyone slowly, in our own sweaty skins, like poached eggs. I open my car, go around and roll down all four windows, curse the air conditioner that gave out two months ago.

Twenty minutes later I'm sitting on the garage-sale couch I bought a week ago to replace the Ethan Allen one my ex-husband stole, along with all my underwear that he forgot to take out of the top dresser drawer and put on the floor when he was cleaning out our house.

Just for the hell of it, I remind myself I own a house in North Carolina. Christ, life can turn on a dime! On the drive home, I tried not to think about the house, the extra money, but I couldn't help myself and decided as soon as I can sell the house, I'm going to move to a better apartment, or maybe even buy another home and get my car air-conditioning fixed.

I dig in my purse and find the orange tip envelope I picked up right before I left work. It feels fatter than normal and for one brief moment I feel joy. A big tip day, the phone call to Ron Tanner. What more could a girl want?

A twenty, a ten and two ones are wrapped around a pink paper. I unfold it. It's one of those weak-ass carbon copies of a layoff notice—*Reduction In Staff*—signed by Joe Gamino, the dickhead.

Great! Stunned, yet not surprised since I've known he's been after me for months, I go to the fridge and grab a Coors Light, twist off the top, listen to it sigh then take a big swig.

Over at the window, I pull back the thin drapes and rest the cool amber beer bottle against my cheek. Fired! Crap.

To make myself feel better, I think about the house in Greensville, how maybe it will sell quickly. It's just got to.

When I was five my parents moved back to Greensville for two weeks, and we stayed at Magnolia Hall until our apartment was ready. I remember the house was white with bricks, really big and filled with antiques. At night my mother, father and I, along with my uncle, would sit on the porch that wrapped around the front. I played on the steps with my doll or ran out into the grass, trying to catch fireflies while the grown-ups' whispers floated through the air.

After we moved into an apartment, and as my mother was unpacking the last box, she started crying and couldn't seem to stop. Two days later my father announced we were going back to California, where it was cool in the summer, warm in winter, and maybe it would be a place where my mother might get her sanity back.

I never understood this two-week, six-thousand-mile trek; it is one of those mythical family stories that children aren't allowed to enter, just watch from the outside and wonder about.

Most of all I remember the cool morning air feathering my face, touching the trees as the three of us walked to our car, me in between my mother, who was crying softly, and Dad, his hand wrapped around mine. I felt wounded for them that day, like now, aching and not knowing why, afraid of the unknown.

I let the drape fall, take another sip of beer and, for the first time in many months, I admit my life has turned to pure crap.

CHAPTER 2

Magnolia Hall
Greensville, NC
June 2000

Ron Tanner and I are in his black BMW headed down a magnolia-lined, gravel driveway. It's been three days since I got fired from the Golden Nugget. That night I ended up drinking the last four beers in the fridge, sitting on the couch, in a beer-hazed stupor for, I guess, about an hour thinking about how my life had not *just* turned to crap, but how it had always been crap and I needed to do something about it. Leanne's words kept thumping through my mind. How I'd get ripped off if I didn't go back to sell the house. And I'm tired of people pissing on me.

I nodded off on the couch, then stumbled to bed, didn't bother to take off my black pants and white dealer's shirt until twelve the next day. When I got up, I walked down to

the 7-Eleven and called the Golden Nugget, asked to speak
to the blackjack pit boss and when Joe answered, I whispered, "You asshole," then hung up, my hand shaking a little. I knew it was stupid and immature, but I did feel better.

I went home, brushed my teeth then sat on the couch
wondering how I was going to pay the rent and feed myself.
I dug in my purse and found my checkbook, thumbed
through the register. Ten minutes later, and a hundred-and-
eighteen dollars overdrawn from a subtraction error I'd made
standing in line at Walgreen's, I put my checkbook back in
my purse.

I had one credit card that wasn't maxed out and the thir-
ty-two dollars I'd left on the coffee table. Without changing clothes, I slung my purse over my shoulder, walked back
to the pay phone, called the Delta eight-hundred number,
got a flight for $694.50, leaving at six-thirty the next morn-
ing, with a two-hour layover in Des Moines. Then I called
Ron, the lawyer. I told him I'd be in Greensville tomorrow
and could he pick me up from the airport? He put me on
hold, came back and said he would, and that it was a good
idea I was coming.

Now Magnolia Hall, a two-story brick house with white-
trimmed porch and dull green shutters, sits at the end of the
lane, looking much smaller than I remember.

I glance over at Ron. He doesn't look like I thought he

would, either. His black hair is cut short—I expected longer blond, for some reason. I guess because the last man I saw in Greensville had blond hair. It's funny what our memories become and what they do to our perceptions.

Ron stops in the circle driveway, in front of the house. Closer, I can see someone has painted the bricks to make it look like the house still has green shutters. He shuts down the engine. The digital clock stays on—it's three-thirty.

I stare through the tinted window, try to remember more about this house, but can't. Ron gets out, comes around and opens my door.

"Thanks." He's parked in the shade of a huge magnolia and it's relatively cool. There's no breeze, no noise.

"This is it," I say, glancing around. The yard is overgrown.

"Yes."

"It's pretty run-down."

"I talked to the housekeeper. She said Mr. Alexander fell on hard times before he died. You never heard from him?"

"No." I leave out that I might not have recognized the man if he had a sign around his neck on a deserted street. I'm sure Ron has heard too many stories, him being an attorney and all. I cross the yard to the porch, climb the stairs, turn around. Huge trees surround the house, cut the ground from the cloudless sky. The air smells green—unfamiliar, and

I wish I could dig up more memories to take me back to the last time I was here, but it's impossible. I was too little and it's been so long. Besides, thirty-five years in a desert town has imprinted dust and cement on my soul.

Ron pulls my black carry-on out of the trunk.

"I'll get that," I say, feeling embarrassed I forgot my suit-case. He shakes his head, carries it up to the front door.

"Want me to put it inside?" He nods toward the door.

"No, thanks. It's not heavy."

Ron's face is tan. I'd guess he's about forty-five. Really mainstream America, clean-cut. Father and mother proba-bly still play golf at some expensive country club, his two brothers, maybe a sister, all have families, dogs, the works.

He's loosened his tie enough so he could undo the top button on his white-and-blue oxford shirt, but he hasn't. I bet his wife picks up his shirts from the cleaners every Wednesday. She's probably someone he met in college, who put him through law school by teaching third grade and is now in good standing with the Greensville Junior League. But there's no ring on his left hand, not even a tan line.

"I have the key to the house," he says, and digs in his pocket.

"Thanks for picking me up at the airport."

Ron takes his hand out of his pocket. He walks to the edge of the steps, stands across from me. A tiny breeze brings his aftershave to me. It's one of those citrusy, clean kinds. I imagine him splashing it on this morning, standing in front of his bathroom mirror, naked from the waist up, a towel wrapped around his somewhat slim, forty-five-year-old waist.

"This happens every once in a while," he says.

"What?" I look at him. He's staring at me, then he smiles.

"Houses dumped on unsuspecting, long-lost relatives."

I shake my head. "No way."

"I specialize in wills, probate, estate tax. Believe me, this happens. Sometimes there's no immediate family. If the deceased hasn't left a will, then it all goes to the closest relative or the state. Your uncle was lucky he had you."

"I'm not sure how lucky, since he's dead."

We laugh at the same time, and then all of a sudden for some odd reason I think about my mother and when she died two years ago. How I had to sort through her underwear, wonder if I should put her Hanes size-seven briefs in the Goodwill bag. I decided that her underwear being worn by a homeless woman who lived one block off Main Street in a cardboard box was too sad. So through guilty feelings, I threw the crotch-stained nylon panties in the kitchen trash.

"One relative is better than none. But too many can make for big problems," Ron says.

I smile. "Never had that problem. As you know my family's pretty small—really nonexistent." I look up and notice the white trim under the porch roof is flaking badly. On the airplane I let myself daydream of what I'd find, all the while telling myself that doing it was dangerous. Yet I let my imagination dredge up an out-of-focus, black-and-white photograph—a large house—breathtaking, like in one of those happy movies, easy to sell, a cash deal.

Ron's voice cuts in. "I did a complete search. There was your uncle's sister, who passed away years ago, and your father. That's it."

My mother's monotone voice had always told me thin stories about strange ex-in-laws. She had acted as if I wasn't related to them, as if I'd only been issued from her.

Ron's cell phone, in his slacks pocket, rings. Bill and I both had cell phones when we first got married. We'd call each other all the time until we couldn't pay the bill.

"Your pocket's ringing," I say, and then wonder why I said something so stupid.

He laughs, checks the caller ID then looks at me. "Mind if I take this?"

"No, go ahead." It's probably his wife, the one who doesn't make him wear a ring, checking in, seeing if he'll be home for dinner.

He walks to the other side of the battered porch, clicks

a button and begins talking. And I'm glad I don't have to say anything for a few minutes.

I push my hair back. My face is sweaty. I look out into the yard. There are no houses close, just magnolias and overgrown bushes, dirty brown with dead spring blooms. This land has to be worth something.

"Sorry about that," Ron says as he walks back. "Major problem with a client. I should get back to the office."

"Thanks for bringing me out here." I glance around. "You said there was a car?"

"Carport is at the back of the house. I never gave you the house keys." He digs into his other pocket, finds a set of keys. "Buick Riviera, 1977. Eighty thousand miles. A cream puff. I came over after you called and started it. Even has air. Drove it to charge the battery. If you want to sell it, I'm sure you'll find a buyer."

"I want to sell it." I take the keys. They swing, glint, hit my palm.

"House key's the one with the red yarn tied in a bow. I think your uncle's housekeeper did that."

I pick it out while Ron walks down the steps. He turns around. "I had my secretary arrange for a county inspection late this afternoon. Every house over a hundred years old in Guilford County has to be inspected before it's put on the market."

"Do you think it'll pass?"

"I don't know. They're pretty stringent these days."

"I hashed out a plan on the airplane—sell the house or at least sign with a Realtor that I trust and get back to Vegas."

"Sounds like a workable plan. The county wants to save the historical homes, so the owner is responsible for repairs. That way when it's sold, the buyer knows what they're getting into. You have my card. Call if you have any questions, problems. I'll need you to sign the probate papers when they're finished, which should be in the next couple of days."

"What about your fee?" I just finished paying six hundred dollars for my latest divorce. God only knows what a probate attorney costs.

"My billing clerk will get in touch with you when everything is assessed."

"Great." I watch as he walks to his car, climbs in. He's tall, well built and moves with confidence. I go to the front door, try again to remember standing on this porch but can't. I slide the key in the lock, turn it the wrong way then back again. The dead bolt clunks open, and I seize the knob and open the door.

"This wall has to be fixed."

"Fixed! Why? It looks fine to me," I say.

Clay, the Guilford County inspector, is running his finger down the bedroom wall. I've been following him for the past thirty minutes, hoping—no, wishing—the house passes inspection. And now, it looks like I'm not going to get what I want.

"See this green line? Mildew. Happens all the time Rain seeps in and mildew takes over just like that." Clay snaps his fingers.

I squint, barely able to see the mossy green line. "Are you sure? Maybe it's just a stain."

He looks at me and grunts. "Lady, I've been doing this kind of work for a very long time. This is mildew."

Half-moon sweat stains are rising on his blue work shirt. The house is hot, stuffy. I didn't have time to open windows, if they'll open. And Clay has informed me of many other things. Greensville is experiencing a heat wave, the likes of which the folks here haven't seen in fifty years. Some have dropped over from the heat. I expect Clay to be one of them any minute. He's also told me outsiders, mostly Northerners, are coming down in droves—with this information, he gave me a sidelong look—building in the area has exploded, and more important, Magnolia Hall is a dump.

Clay thumbs through papers on his clipboard then searches in his back pocket, finds a white handkerchief and mops his forehead.

"If you plan on selling your house anytime soon you can forget it."

"Look, can't you just sign off? The green line is barely there." I move closer to the wall. "I swear it's so small you—"

"Underneath there's trouble. Doesn't seem like much from the outside. Can't give you the okay until the wall's cleaned up. You're darned fortunate that's all that's wrong, the way this place has been let go."

Resolved, I step back. "How do you fix something like that?"

"The way the town's growing, it'll take you a month of Sundays to get someone out here. Does that air conditioner work?" Clay nods to the old unit clinging to the windowsill.

"I don't know." I walk over, find the On switch and push it in. Nothing. I look at Clay. His lips press together.

"Preventative maintenance, that's the key to these old houses."

"I inherited this place. That wall," I say, "sounds like a major expense. I have less than zero money." I don't know why I'm telling him this, for God's sake. What does he care?

Clay taps the checklist. "Depends on what you consider major. Some of those new construction companies charge a lot. First thing with mildew is you gotta get to the problem. From what I can tell, it's coming from the window." He walks over to the window, three feet from the mildew, runs his hand over the sill. "I'm surprised the one with the air-conditioning unit isn't leaking. Best thing to do is seal all the way around, that'll stop more damage, then when the wall's replaced make sure they seal it up real tight."

"Wall replaced?"

"Gotta take down part of the plasterboard." Clay taps one of the dull white-and-green magnolias that make up the wallpaper.

"Christ! I don't have the time or money for this."

"You aren't a Southern gal, are you?"

"No."

Clay looks at me like he's about to take pity on me. "You can buy caulk at Home Depot. Probably only take half a tube." He shakes his head. "After the drywall's taken down, they'll wash the wood to get rid of the mildew then put up new drywall, tape, paint or wallpaper."

"Right," I say, but feel overwhelmed. "How much do you think this is gonna cost?"

"'Bout eight hundred dollars."

"Oh, God!"

A bead of sweat trickles down my forehead into my right eye, and I blink, wipe at it, know I'm smearing my mascara.

"Plaster dust gets into everything and there's nothing you can do about that. Make sure whoever does the job puts Visqueen up."

"Are you sure I can't buy some Lysol and wipe down the wall? I'll seal the window."

"No. When it's gone this far, you can't. It's like the silent killer of walls."

"Shit. The silent killer, ha-ha."

"Just sign on the line."

I take the blue pen and clipboard that says Guilford County and look at the small-print form. It's smudged with Clay's sweat, now mine. "There's no other way?"

Clay looks at me like I might be trying to bribe him. I laugh.

"Something funny?"

I study the paper. "Am I signing my life away?"

He straightens a little. His face is red, more sweaty than mine. I changed into shorts and T-shirt after Ron left, thank God, but now they're sticking to my skin. As soon as Clay is gone I'm going to open windows, drink some water.

"Your signature acknowledges you're aware of this infraction and that you'll be in compliance before you sell."

"Right. And what if I'm not?"

His eyebrow rises. "County can sue you."

"Guess I won't go there." I write my name, wish I would have asked the judge who granted me my quickie divorce to change my name back to one I can stand.

"Okay, that's about all. When you get the repairs done, give me a call." He hands me a copy of the paper I've just signed, takes back his pen and points to a phone number in the right-hand corner. "If I'm not there just leave a message."

I nod, walk to the edge of the doorway and look back. Clay is still writing. The room is empty except for a four-poster bed with white sheets and a yellow blanket. I look at the wall and realize I could easily begin to hate this house. He finishes, clips his pen in his shirt pocket, holds the clipboard like a football and walks toward the door.

"Don't feel bad about the mildew. Lots of folks have problems and don't even know about them."

"Lucky them."

Hemsley House
Greensville, NC
March 1861

I am to marry James Alexander in three days!

Father insists we not wait. He stated clearly he believes Mr. Alexander to be the right choice. Thankfully, Father didn't mention I have not had any other proposals and that is why I am expected to marry James Alexander.

When my father announced what he wanted for me, I stamped my foot and fussed. Mama ushered me to my room, and informed me I will behave like a lady and a dutiful daughter. I did not tell her I don't want a "lord and master" to honor and obey, for I knew then as I know now, my words would not change her or Father's mind.

More than anything my parents want their only daughter to be a wife. As my father clearly stated, he and my brother do not need an old maid in this house and on their hands.

Months back, when I arrived at the age of eighteen, I heard my parents discussing with much trepidation that their eldest would not find a husband if she remained so quiet.

I am not quiet! I am just not very social. I don't understand myself sometimes. I do not like to go to parties like other girls. I have always liked to read, write letters, write in my diary. My parents do not believe this behavior is good for their aging daughter.

"Who will marry her?" they whispered to each other in not so gentle whispers.

Then, three days ago after Mr. Alexander asked for my hand, they decided I should accept his proposal. The next day, when neither would listen to me, I started sobbing. I ran up to my room, stood by the window and thought about leaping to the ground. Maybe my bones would break, then they would listen.

I imagined my body drifting out the window, lifting up into the air then plunging through the warm Carolina sunshine, like a bird in flight. I felt the air on my face, the breeze fanning my ankles as I leaned out farther.

Suddenly I knew I could not smash myself on the ground. However, I remained by the window until the sky was silvery and sugar-strewn with moonlight.

After Father had gone to bed, Mama came to see me. Her face was drawn, her mouth tight. Her fingers touched my hairline, smoothed it back from my temples. She spoke softly, claiming that it would be much easier on all of us if I accepted my fate. Father was doing what was best for me, and I needed to trust in him and the Lord.

I seized her hand and asked if she could do what I had to do, marry someone she wasn't sure she loved, someone she hardly knew. She tried to laugh, then breathed in deeply, brought her hand to her throat.

"Charlotte, don't make yourself weak trying to be happy. If you do not hate Mr. Alexander, you might love him one day, like I do your father."

I do admire Mr. Alexander. We became acquainted a year ago, a month after he moved to Greensville. He always has a kind look about him. He told me he likes to read history books, then he smiled a nice smile. And his laughter brought to mind the large church bell ringing across Greensville on a Sunday morning.

Yet my heart never pounds hard in my chest like I heard other girls say their hearts do when they are around someone they are fond of. I know I do not love him.

Will I ever love him? I do not know. Mama told me not to worry about married love, it will surely find me. And as long as I'm a good wife to Mr. Alexander, that is all that matters.

In the past few weeks, Mama has schooled me on how to handle the servants, how to plan meals and tell the cook what to prepare. All the general ways to keep a home. She also whispered in my ear there are certain other obligations I will have as a wife. Then suddenly she pulled back, her round face pale as a magnolia blossom, her lips flat against each other. She fanned herself with her hand.

"You'll find out soon enough, oh, Heavenly Father!"

Soon she left my side, marched down the stairs and called in a high-pitched voice for her servant, Isabell. I know the obligations she whispered are what the other, more sophisticated girls giggle about—the duty of a wife. Some say these duties are very uncomfortable.

Night after night, I sit by my window and wonder how I will feel when my life as a—

Mama came in and I hid this book in the folds of my

skirt. She would be very upset to know I've been writing before my wedding. Many, along with Father, believe writing leads to worry for young ladies.

I would think she would be desolate that Mr. Alexander is building a home miles from town and I will live so far away. When I hint at these fears, Mama shakes her head and claims I am a true Southern girl, one who is too attached to her family and someday I will be happy and not want to come home.

This morning Mama found me sitting by the window, tears dried upon my cheeks. She said very sternly that I must grow up and start a family of my own because it will soon be time to have babies. I feel like cloth being torn and readied for a wedding dress. I pray James Alexander is a patient man, for he will have to be with his new bride. He will need years of tolerance, because it is difficult for me to imagine myself old and stooped over and still his wife with adult children, if the Lord sees fit to give us their souls.

I do not understand fate, my life, and said so to Mama. She told me I think too much for a young woman. I should trust in Father's decision. The Lord's purpose is to make me a wife—what I was born for. Try as hard as I might, I do not believe this. Yet, I am now resolved that in three days, Mr. Alexander will be my lord and master for eternity. Tonight as I contemplate giving up everything that is familiar, I do not believe eighteen is so very old.

CHAPTER 3

Magnolia Hall
Greensville, NC
June 2000

Clay climbs in his white utility truck, starts the almost soundless engine and rolls up the window. Then he leans over and fiddles with the air-conditioning. He looks back, doesn't smile. Why couldn't he have just signed off on the inspection? My life would be a lot easier.

I walk back into the house. Late-afternoon sunlight races down the hallway before I close the door, turning the scratched oak floor, for a moment, into a gleaming lake.

Two summers ago, four weeks after we met, Bill and I spent a July week on Lake Mead, right outside Las Vegas. We rented a houseboat at the marina, packed the boat's kitchen with sliced ham, soft wheat bread, Swiss cheese, medium-priced merlot, three six-packs of Coors, bottled water and my new CD player.

I have to admit we were in a sexual frenzy, and this trip only increased it. Lake Mead, a man-made lake, is a breathtaking lie, and in the summer the air is hot, dry—like another planet that's closer to the sun.

That week Bill drank all the beer and most of the wine. The idea I'd found the perfect person made me drunk with happiness—who needed booze? What I didn't know then was I should have drunk myself into a stupor, jumped overboard and swum to shore. But of course I fooled myself into believing the relationship was just right. I was blind to the truth. Bill shoved signs in my face that he was a shit-heel right from the beginning. In the houseboat-rental office, he claimed he'd forgotten his credit card and I let myself overlook that tired old excuse! I paid for the entire trip, as if I were some rich broad with a gigolo. I knew he was a con artist. I really did, but I lied to myself.

I walk into Magnolia Hall's living room and drag my toe across one of the carpet dents where a piece of furniture used to rest. I pull the white sheer curtain back, yank on the roll-up window shade and expect a cloud of dust.

There isn't any. The fading sunlight showers the room in pink hues, accenting the emptiness. I turn the old window locks out, lift the window. Moist, cooler air floats in, bellows the curtains around my legs.

Two brocade chairs sit in the middle of the room and look like old ladies who have forgotten to leave. I must have been in this room when I was little, but I don't remember.

After Ron left, before the inspection from hell took place, I walked around the house, and I'm still astounded that there is hardly any furniture in the house. Magnolia Hall is shaped like a two-story box with a hallway running down the middle. Downstairs there are two front rooms, this one and the one across the hall. That room only contains a sagging green couch.

Behind it is a library or office with floor-to-ceiling bookcases where five tired books stand on one shelf. There's a rocking chair in the corner by one of the windows. Across the hall a dining-room table and three chairs stand polished, ready, lonely except for a small hutch.

Upstairs there are three bedrooms, two of them completely bare. The huge bathroom has a claw-foot bathtub, no shower. A blue towel and three bars of Ivory soap, still in their wrappers, are stacked neatly on the back of the toilet.

And there's no trace of Grey Alexander.

I looked in the medicine chest and the old white chest by the door. Nothing. What happened to the man's razor, comb, shampoo? And his clothes? It's as if he never lived here. I expected piles of things, or at least some pictures, something to prove he was alive.

The living room curtain fans against my legs again. I walk back to the kitchen, touch the dead rotary phone that sits on a tiny table. There's something very ironic in the fact that I'm still going to have, to haul my ass down to the local convenience store because I don't have a working phone.

I walk to the room with the bookcases and notice the fireplace is immaculate. At one of the bookcases, I draw my finger on a shelf. There's no dust. I trace the spines of all five books. I pull out the *Mark Twain Anthology*, look at the bookmark. It's a picture of a man with light hair, straight nose and thin lips. He's wearing a tuxedo, a white pleated shirt and bow tie. On the back is written in pencil "Grey Alexander." In this picture, he looks like I remember my father looked the last time I saw him thirty-four years ago. My heart hurts a little.

Grey's hair is cut just so, his tie so straight. I wonder how he could ignore the upstairs mildewed wall, and why isn't there more of him in this house? His silent black-and-white eyes stare back at me.

Magnolia Hall
March 1861

It has been two weeks since I was married and my husband brought me to his new home. I try not to think about how far I have come in these few short weeks. I miss so much—my mother and father, my room, the house I lived in since the day I was born. I also miss the mornings in Greensville, the soft footsteps of servants around Hemsley. I am so sick with feelings of loss I do not know what to do.

I did my best to hide my feelings the day Mr. Alexander and I left Greensville after the wedding, but Mama detected my sadness as I was dressing. She petted my hair and told me my life would be fine someday. I looked up at her, asked how she knew, how she could be so very sure.

With my question she straightened as if something had come over her and announced I was acting foolish, I was a married woman, with a good husband and I should be happy, and if I were not, I was to find some way to make myself happy—I was to endure. Then she sat down beside me as if she could not make up her mind, either, took my hand in hers, and said she would always love me, but for her sake I had to endure until I found a way to be happy.

I asked why Father wanted me to go away, why was it so important that I wed.

Mama shook her head, studied my fingers for a moment too long.

"That is just the way our lives are. Father wants you married, and you do not seem capable of choosing a husband or even finding and keeping a suitor. You are too shy, Charlotte. Reservedness is becoming—however, you are very queer in your actions."

I have always lived away from people. I do not know why. I feel a distance at times. I am not one for change or exciting events. I have always liked to stay home, be in the same place. I love a room when I have been in it a thousand times. I adored the everyday view from my window.

My husband and I are different in that way. Mr. Alexander seems joyful with the house he built. He talks about the newness of the entry hall and the sitting room, the fine dining room and library. How, over time, he will bring new and beautiful things to our new home.

The house is beautiful. Late in the afternoon, when the front door is open, sunlight turns the floor to glistening silk. I saw happiness burst forth on my husband's face yesterday afternoon when he walked through the front door and the house was ablaze with sunset.

Two nights ago after dinner, my husband asked me into the parlor. I went in thinking he wanted to discuss

the management of the house or the night's menu—
that the greens were bitter or the bread was too tough.

He sat next to me on the divan, took my hand in his.
In the firelight his eyes looked bluer than I have ever
seen them. I asked him if he were displeased about my
management of the house, the kitchen?

"No, I am not." Then he said very quickly, "I worry
you are not happy."

I blinked, looked down at my lap, embarrassed that
my feelings are so transparent.

"Charlotte, you must always be truthful. I am your
husband and you must be honest with me."

I could only nod.

"I do not want you to be sad and I sense that you
are, Charlotte." And then he squeezed my hand. I
dipped my chin more. I did not wish to dampen his
spirits.

"Tell me, Charlotte."

And suddenly words began to pour out of me.

"My sorrow for what I used to know is great, silly as
that is. I am afraid this makes me a very selfish person."

His arm went around my shoulders and we sat silent-
ly.

A moment later he stood, announced that he would
retire to the library, he had much work to do. He kissed

my forehead and I was alone and could think more clearly.

I watched the flames of the fire, forced myself to remember how long ago I attended the Greensville sewing circles with Mama. There I heard women professing their adoration for their husbands, and I began hoping to experience the same kind of union. I am still praying some wifely devotion will find me—make me tremble on the veranda when my husband appears from the foggy mist.

Last night Mr. Alexander and I were sitting out on the veranda, and he told me in a delicate way how much he has loved me from the moment his eyes fell upon me at the evening party my parents hosted. With the night breeze fanning my warm face, I smiled.

"Thank you, for the very dear compliment, Mr. Alexander."

"Why don't you refer to me as James, it being a more familiar, loving term?"

When I did not answer, he stood and stared down at me.

Why didn't I tell him the truth—that I am blind to what a wife should feel or do for her husband. The sadness in his eyes told me he knew, yet he did not press me. Late that night when he held me close and whispered promises to me, I felt dizzy and wondered what it will be like to spend the rest of my life in his arms.

But I did not say a word.

Magnolia Hall
Greensville, NC
June 2000

"Good holy God!"

A black woman is standing on the back porch with her face pressed against the kitchen screen door and my heart is thumping into my throat.

"You shouldn't use the Lord's name in vain," she says, and straightens a little.

"What? What do you want?" I ask, then step back and wonder if there's a knife close by. I came into the kitchen this morning hoping to find coffee, maybe tea. But there was nothing. And now this!

The woman laughs and puts her hands on her hips. "Why, child, don't you remember me? I'm Tildy Butler."

Tight black curls lie in swirls close to her head. She smiles again and her teeth, very white and perfect, take up a lot of her unfamiliar face.

"Hope I didn't scare you." She opens the screen, comes into the kitchen. "I was going to call and then I remembered the phone had been shut down, so I thought, well, Tildy Butler, you are acting inhospitable. Then I decided I needed to come right over and see Miss Juliette."

I take a step back and wish my heart would quit beating so hard. "Who did you say you are?"

She gives me an up-down look. "My, you look the same. A little bigger, but you're still that pretty little blond child. How are you, Miss Juliette?"

"I'm afraid—"

"You don't remember me? I was hoping you would. No one likes to be forgotten. I'm Tildy, your uncle's housekeeper. I met you a long time ago. Remember?"

"Oh…yes," I say, because I do remember that my uncle had a housekeeper, but I don't remember this woman specifically.

She smiles, nods. "My, it's good to have you back. My friend Sara found out you were in town through her brother-in-law's son who works for the attorney who's taking care of Mr. Grey's things. I hear he's a very nice man. She called me right away, told me I'd better get over here and help you out."

I mentally follow the trail. "Oh."

"Honey, it's so good to see you."

"Thank you." I finally offer my hand, but she brushes it away and her arms go around me. She feels smaller than she looks and smells like lemons or bleach, maybe a mixture of the two.

"Honey, it's been so long." She pats my back then lets go, steps back.

"It has."

"And what? You're twenty now?" She laughs, her head back, her hand over her heart.

"More like forty."

"Thirty-five years? Seems like yesterday. It's about time you came home. I'm so happy I get to tend you and Magnolia Hall. Why, I've been missing you both."

"What?"

"Why, honey, you can't take care of the house all by yourself. This place needs me, like you do. Everybody needs some help now and then." Tildy claps her hands as a child would, and through the screen I see a cardinal dart from the tree and disappear.

I blink. "I'm leaving soon, selling the house."

"I've taken care of all the owners of Magnolia Hall, I couldn't stop with you."

She turns, goes out to the porch and comes back with a shopping bag and places it in the corner by the refrigerator. "Brought some food. Didn't think you would have time to go to the market. Isn't it a beautiful summer morning? You're going to love it here."

"I'm only staying until I can list with a Realtor," I say again.

Her head turns a little like a dog hearing a high-pitched whistle. "I grew up in this kitchen. Know Magnolia Hall like the back of my hand."

I suddenly realize I'm tired. I didn't sleep well last night, between thinking about the wall, wondering how the hell I'm going to get it repaired when I don't have any money or space left on my credit cards. Then, about one in the morning, I started wondering where I'm going to find another dealing job when I get back to Vegas. After all that, sleeping wasn't an option. Besides, the house is noisy with groans and cracks—probably more structural problems.

"Mr. Grey always talked about your daddy. He was crazy about his brother. It's too bad he couldn't come home much. And then when we lost him, why it was like losing Charlotte all over again." Tildy smiles, nods.

Charlotte. My mother would sit on the couch, full glass in one hand, cigarette in the other. She always described how my father's family had canonized Charlotte, his sister. *Charlotte this, Charlotte that, only because she died so young.*

"I'm sorry about your daddy. Didn't see him much after Charlotte passed, but we still loved him. Mr. Grey always said his brother needed to come home. Now his daughter has. How's your mama? I knew her, too. Not well, but when they moved back to Greensville for that brief time, she seemed so nice. Very pretty, like a movie star."

"She passed away a couple of years ago," I say, then add, "liver cancer."

Tildy's eyes widen. "I'm so sorry. I didn't know." She leans forward. "My goodness, you're an orphan now."

I blink. I'd never thought of myself like that. But she's right, I am. "Yes, I guess so."

"That's why it's good you've come home. This is where you belong. Everything's going to be all right now."

It would take a million bucks to make my life all right, but I don't say this. "This isn't my home."

Tildy crosses the room, digs through her shopping bag, pulls out a cooked chicken wrapped in plastic. "Thought I'd make some chicken salad. That's always good in the summer. Cool, refreshing. When I heard Magnolia Hall was yours I was so thankful. Mr. Grey wasn't much for contacting people. I told him he ought to call you, but he always said he'd do it later. Then it was too late for later."

She opens the fridge, clucks her tongue, finds the plug and sticks it in the electrical socket. A giant hum grinds through the room.

"Thank the good Lord the electricity is on. You get it turned on?"

I shake my head. "No, the lawyer must have."

"Nice man to be worrying about all that."

"He's getting paid as soon as I sell the house." I look around, laugh. I'm standing in a strange kitchen, talking to a woman I don't know, about people who, after this, I will never see again, and I'm jobless.

"See, you're happy. My, Mr. Grey loved people to be happy at Magnolia Hall. And he loved this house like she was one of his relatives. So he'd want you to have her. You know he would."

"I don't know that. He hadn't seen me in thirty-five years."

"Honey, you're family. That's all that matters."

Tildy walks to the large stack of paper plates I left on the counter last night, turns back and raises an eyebrow. "These paper things are for picnics, not dining in the house."

"I picked up Chinese last night," I say, but for a moment I feel like a kid who just made a mud pie on the kitchen floor.

Tildy lifts her brow again. "That's no excuse. There's beautiful china and silver for meals, especially supper. Mr. Grey would expect you to use the right dishes. They're yours now."

"I didn't want to dirty the…" I stop, wonder why the hell I'm explaining myself.

"The blue-and-white morning dishes are what you should

use when it's not fancy." She points to the cabinet in front of her. "They're stronger than they look. You need to use the china, child. Why let it go to waste?"

"China! There are only two plates, from what I could see. Unless there's more somewhere else."

Last night I went through the cabinets and drawers. I found the kitchen immaculate but almost empty, like the rest of the house. An old set of pots and pans in the space by the stove, and dishes, two of each piece, were stacked neatly in the cabinet next to the sink.

"Quality, not quantity, is important. The best dishes are in the dining room." Tildy raises her arms a little, as if she's announcing this information to a crowd.

"I looked in there. There are only two plates."

"Your next meal, you should eat off the china, honey. We use the blue-and-white before five. The Minton for dinner and supper, the Adams for holidays."

"Mrs. Butler, I'm fine. When I'm home I use paper all the time. Really, I'm from Las Vegas, we're very informal out there."

My apartment has crappy garage-sale furniture, plastic forks I stole from the casino coffee shop—and now I wish I had taken more—paper napkins and cheap orange plastic plates I bought at Sam's Club.

"My name's Tildy, really Matilda is my given, but everyone calls me Tildy. You can do the same, honey."

She turns as if I haven't said a word and reseals the paper plates then crosses the kitchen and puts them on a shelf in the pantry and comes back smiling.

"You are just gonna love Magnolia Hall. I'll help you. Talk in town is the county might be taking the house for back taxes if they couldn't find any family to come home.

"Back taxes?"

"Oh, they're paid up. I was thinking last night if you don't have a lot of cash we can go to garage sales and pick up a few things, maybe paint. Everything's better when you take care of—"

"Tildy, I'm going back to Las Vegas just as soon as I can. And now I have to worry about back taxes."

She stares at me for a moment like I've turned a cold hose on her, but then she shakes her head.

"Honey, that back-tax thing was just a rumor. In case they didn't find you. I know Mr. Grey paid them up. And you'll change your mind about leaving. We'll do some of the fixing up. New curtains in here would be nice. I saw some daisy curtains with scalloped edges at The Big K over off Market Street. They'd look real fine at that window—not too expensive, either."

I rub my tongue against the back of my teeth and wonder what I should say, wonder if she's got a screw loose. But before I can think of anything, she starts up again.

"Mr. Grey didn't know how to add the feminine touches around here. Now you and I can make the changes we need to. Might take some time, but we'll get it all done. Some people don't realize that a little bit every day makes a world of difference, makes a person feel at home. Soon you got a whole big pile of good in front of you."

"I can't stay. I'm going home."

"Magnolia Hall is your family home. Now you have to take care of her. You don't give back a gift. A gift is a gift!"

"He didn't give me the house! It's mine because I'm the only one left!"

"It's all the same. You are the rightful owner."

"I'm selling the house just as soon as I can. You wouldn't want to buy it, would you?"

"Goodness, no. I don't have that kind of money after I put my child through school. You gonna sell it as soon as you can?"

"The wall upstairs didn't pass the county inspection."

"I knew it wouldn't. Mr. Grey was sick the last few years. We didn't have much time for fixing. I took care of him till his dying day. Then Jeff Hollis, fine young police officer, came out and locked up the place. That was the very first time after Miss Charlotte and Mr. James built her nobody lived here. Mr. Grey used to talk about the first Miss Charlotte all the time."

"My father's sister?"

"No, he talked about her, too, but I'm talking about your great-great-great, oh, you know a long time ago, her husband, James Alexander built this house in 1860. Your daddy's sister was named after her."

"Oh." I look around and think about how much I don't know about this family.

"Now you're here. Too bad you didn't get back before your uncle died."

"I didn't know he was sick."

"That's right. I told him to call you. Your daddy would have told you, though, if he was still here."

"I didn't have any contact with my father, either." I say, and cross my arms.

"My land, your daddy was such a nice man."

"I wouldn't know about—"

"I remember years ago, when he came home for three weeks in the spring. Told me you'd moved to Nevada with your mama. He seemed so sad. I've never been there. Actually I've never been out of the state."

"Maybe you should travel," I say, but I'm thinking of my father and wondering why he never wanted to share me with his family.

"Are you married?" Tildy glances at my left hand.

"Not anymore."

"Oh, child. I'm sorry."

I realize Tildy is the first person to say this to me. People in Las Vegas expect divorce—don't think anything about a marriage dissolving into lies and crap.

"It was for the better. I couldn't afford the man's bad habits."

Tildy touches my hand for a moment. Her skin is cooler than I expect. "Honey, everything is going to be okay. You just wait and see."

CHAPTER 4

Magnolia Hall
Greensville, NC
June 2000

I'm staring at Grey Alexander's picture. Weird, I know, but after I spent a half hour trying to convince Tildy I can't let her work here because I have no money to pay her and there's really not much for her to do, I came into the library, picked up the picture I found yesterday. Maybe I was trying to center myself or some damned thing.

The centering thing isn't working. I honestly thought Tildy would agree when I explained there was nothing that needed cleaning. But when she said she couldn't possibly leave me all alone in this house, I knew I wasn't making any headway. Then she told me she could dust the baseboards, mop floors, wipe out the cupboards, cook and, with a big smile on her face, she announced she wanted to keep me company!

I'm still wondering what "keeping me company" means to her. However she brought coffee, cream, sugar with her. She made a pot and the first sip was heaven.

Finally, I gave up trying to convince her to go home. She was blabbing on about family and my father, how he grew up here and she was so fond of him. Maybe that's why I wandered into the library and picked up Grey's picture.

"Your head hurting you?"

I look toward the door, and Tildy's voice. "No, I'm fine."

"Your forehead's all wrinkled up like you have a headache."

"I didn't sleep well last night."

"Mr. Grey never had trouble sleeping. Something bothering you?"

"Not much." I laugh. "I'm only in a strange house, in a strange town. And I have no idea how I'm going to get the wall upstairs repaired so I can sell this place and get back to my life."

"It's gotta be more than that."

"Isn't that enough? Think if you had to go out to Vegas, didn't know any one."

"What you got there?"

"It's a picture of Grey. I found it yesterday." I stare at it. "He looks like my father—at least what I remember."

"Yes, they do resemble each other. But they were different. Mr. Grey, why, he loved this house and the idea of family. He was a real Southerner."

"And my father?" A wave of regret washes over me. I don't want to know any more. My father left me years ago and I don't know anything about him.

"As I recall, he always wanted to go away, travel. He joined the air force when Mr. Grey begged him not to. Mr. Grey even found a way to get him out of what he signed. Then he met your mama on leave in California. When your daddy came back with you and your mama, he just seemed restless, like he needed to get away again. And your mama was a mess. She didn't like it here. Said she was homesick, missed the ocean. So off you all went."

My mother was full of contradictions. Although she claimed to love the ocean, she never went back after she and my father split. She kept huge, full boxes that had been opened and closed too many times. Every Thanksgiving she would rustle through them, show me sparkling dresses, memory after memory. She'd hold up a blue velvet and sigh, then explain how pretty she looked when she wore it. I stopped asking questions because she'd never answer any.

Another cardboard box was filled with picture albums. Her fingertips touched the images and she'd say how she wished I looked like her. She never talked about my father, and if I asked, she'd stare at me with those soft blue eyes and shake her head, then mention a time before she married, when her life had hope. She'd hold up her yellowing souvenirs, make up pretty lies, then drop them back in their hiding places.

"Your daddy was different. Mr. Grey loved memories, loved his history." Tildy's words bring me back. "I remember how your mama and daddy used to sit out on the porch, right out there—" her hand kind of flutters toward the front of the house "—and talk about going home. California certainly wasn't your daddy's home. But he seemed to love your mama so much. I guess that's why he went back."

Love.

The idea of my parents loving each other is so foreign to me. When she spoke of my father or his family her voice was always brittle. Yet, I hold one image so clear. It was before they divorced. Right before my father was due to come back from a trip my mother would shower, comb her hair and spray Emerada perfume in a halo around her, then sit on the couch and look out the window, as if she couldn't wait to see him. She always told me it wouldn't be long until his plane landed and he drove up the driveway. Then months later, she packed our bags, climbed into the blue Oldsmobile and drove all night to Las Vegas, not saying a word, just the glow from the dashboard on her Grace Kelly cheekbones, her tight jaw like a cup, holding all her anger.

I look at Tildy. "I don't really care about my father."

A tiny gasp escapes from her. "Sure you do! He's your family. And Mr. Grey loved family, loved this house, his things because they reminded him of family."

I shake my head. "Right! Then why is the house practically empty?" I fan his photograph at her.

Tildy takes the picture, as if to protect it. "That's a real long story. We'll get to that."

"There's nothing personal of his…" I stop. Why am I saying all this? I don't care.

"I cleaned up when he died. I knew you wouldn't want to see his hairbrush, maybe find dandruff in it, his toilet items. He was a very private man. He would have wanted it that way. I wanted you to know the nice things about him, know how orderly he was."

"*Orderly!* He didn't even make a will."

"He thought about living, not dying. Even when your daddy died and we took his ashes to the Greensville family plot, your uncle said your daddy was living in the trees, the grass, the wind. Right after he said those words, an airplane cut a path over us. Not one of those big jets but a little tiny thing, looked like it was just big enough for one person. We all looked up, even the preacher. Mr. Grey said it was a sign from God that James Alexander, your daddy who'd been a pilot all his adult life, was right there with us, and real close to the sky that was so blue."

I try not to laugh but can't help myself. Tildy's big brown eyes widen.

"I'm sorry, that's just so…silly."

"It's the truth."

"I didn't mean it didn't happen. It was probably a coincidence."

She steps back just a little, looks at me. "I thought you'd like that story."

I feel like a shit for saying anything. "I did, really. It's just a lot to take in."

Her hand touches my shoulder then it's gone.

"I know."

"This is the first time I've heard anything about my father's funeral." I shake my head. "What the hell difference does it make? I don't even care, really. I was young."

"Yes, you do. Anybody would."

"How many people attended?"

"Oh, honey, not many. Mr. Grey and Sara and Sara Lee, they're old friends of the family. My Alexandria attended, made me proud. The preacher knew your daddy when he was a little boy, and he read that poem about flying. I only remember a few words—'Oh, I have slipped the surly bonds of earth and'…my land, I can't recall the rest. But it was beautiful."

I close my eyes and remember the poem my father used

to recite when he drove me to kindergarten. I look at Tildy, "'Oh, I have slipped the surly bonds of earth and danced the skies on laughter-silvered wings.'"

"That's it. I thought it was appropriate."

I wonder what it would have been like, standing in a graveyard, watching what was left of my father go into the ground and hearing that poem read by someone else.

"Your daddy would have wanted you there."

"Maybe not." My voice sounds so small. I think about my mother telling me, weeks after my father's death, that he had died. I was fifteen, sitting on the couch by the window, painting my fingernails with Pink Puff Maybelline Fast-Drying Nail Polish. She walked into the living room, stood in front of me, her arms crossed.

"Don't get that on the couch."

"I won't."

"Your father—" she took a long breath "—died."

I looked down and thought, *who?* When I glanced up, she was gone. I could hear her in the kitchen, filling a glass with ice, then vodka and orange juice. I swallowed hard, told myself I needed to cry but couldn't. I felt dead inside. It was as if Peter Jennings had announced one of the cast from a black-and-white sitcom had passed away. I knew the character—but not really.

"Sad things happen in life," Tildy says.

"Did anyone cry?" I imagine myself crying, the wind blowing through my hair, the early May sun practically blinding me as I look up, watch the airplane cut the blue sky.

"I did. Your daddy was nice when we were children. My mama always went on about how Mr. James picked up his clothes and was neat as a pin in the bathroom."

That day my mother told me about my father's death, I got off the couch, heard my mother place the vodka bottle back on the top shelf above the silky green ironstone dishes. I walked into the kitchen, my hands in my pockets, nail polish sticking to my soft blue cotton shorts. I needed her to say something to me.

She was leaning against the white counter, the small of her back pressing against it. The glass rim rested against her red lipsticked lower lip, her eyes dull—flat.

"What should I do?" I asked.

"Nothing. Not one goddamned thing. He never came around, and the funeral is over anyway."

"Mr. Grey didn't believe in death," Tildy says, breaking into my memory. "I don't think he ever accepted Mr. James or Miss Charlotte's death." She studies my uncle's picture. "This was taken a few years back when Mr. Grey used to go out. That was the night of the Sons of the American Revolution annual dinner."

"Sons of the American Revolution? They still have groups like that?"

"Yes. Mr. Grey, he was big into his groups. Liked to carry on the family name. When he got cancer his life was just sliced away, little by little. Every step was a big shock to him and I think up to the very end, he believed it wasn't happening—like maybe it was a bad dream. Magnolia Hall held him tight, but then she had to let him go."

Tildy takes my hand and pats it. "Don't worry. I knew him all my life. He would have wanted you to have this house. You're family. It's like giving it to your daddy—no, more like giving it to his sister, Charlotte. You have to trust in what has happened."

My mind is swimming with all the memories, stories. "What I need is a drink."

"Can I get you some iced tea?"

I laugh, realize my chest aches. "I was thinking about something stronger."

"There's no liquor in the house."

"Maybe that's why my mother was crying." I laugh again, I guess to combat the uneasiness I feel.

Tildy gasps then covers her mouth.

"My mother was an alcoholic. I came to grips with that a long time ago."

Tildy hands me the picture, and I look at it again, feeling like a ship without an anchor.

"There's more of your father in you than your mother," she says.

"Well, he was pretty much an SOB, too."

"You'll find out different. Maybe we shouldn't be talking about this right now. Have you had anything to eat this morning? All that caffeine and no nourishment can make you say things you don't mean. Just like my daughter. Goodness alive, doesn't anyone take care of themselves anymore?"

I lay the picture on the bookshelf. Her hand brushes my elbow and before I can take another breath, the woman guides me to the kitchen.

"It's been a month of Sundays since I had somebody to cook for, take care of. Feels good."

She goes to the kitchen sink and looks out the window. Recognition flashes through my mind. I watched her in this room, years ago, right before we left for California, right before our lives came unglued.

"I'm gonna cook you something real Southern, something so sumptuous your little mouth is going to water—"

"You don't have to cook for me."

Tildy shifts, rests her hands on her lush hips. "I have cooked for everyone in this house. You aren't going to be any different. No arguing. What did you say you did in Las Vegas?"

"I'm a blackjack dealer."

"Well, my, my. You don't look like a blackjack dealer. If you wore glasses, maybe a librarian. They have libraries in Las Vegas?"

I laugh. Everyone from the outside thinks Las Vegas isn't a real town. "Sure."

"So why didn't you become a librarian or a teacher?"

"I don't know."

"Mr. Grey, he loved books and the room he kept them in. So did your daddy."

"It's not much of a library."

Tildy's smile slips away, which makes me feel bad.

"I mean, it's a nice room, and all, but there's only a few books."

"It was a wonderful library long time ago. Every shelf full with all the classics, real comfortable chairs and a sofa that was covered in a beautiful green brocade—don't you remember?"

"No. What happened to all of it?"

"After he got sick, doctors took a lot of the money. He'd let his insurance lapse. The state helped him a little with social security. But to get all the benefits he would have had to give up Magnolia Hall and he wouldn't. So he gave things away."

"Gave them away...how would that help?"

"That's what we called it."

"What? Why?"

"The last Saturday of each month, Mr. Grey had me take something up to an antique store in Mocksville so people around here wouldn't find out."

"So he sold them?"

"We like to think of it as giving them away. The man had his pride. After a while, the owner came down here with a truck, every third Saturday of the month. It was so sad to see bits of Mr. Grey's life slipping out that door, like ham on a cutter—one thin piece after another. I don't think he died of the cancer. Giving up all his family possessions was what really killed him."

"Maybe he would have been smarter to sell the house, buy a nice condo, go on vacation. Not worry about this place, his memories."

Tildy looks around like she's not listening. "It's a better day with you here. Don't you worry, this house is gonna be just fine. It always survives."

She's serious. "As soon as I get the bedroom wall fixed, I'm going to list with—"

"I told Mr. Grey he shouldn't put off fixing that wall. Said he'd do it when he had time. Then he didn't have no more time, no more money."

"Do you know anyone who might repair the wall?"

"I can check around, but, honey, Magnolia Hall's never been *sold*. Any of your mama's family out there in Nevada? Or a boyfriend that might help you?"

"No and no." I make check marks in the air with my right index finger.

"Then that's not much of a home to go back to."

"But it's where I live, work. I can't deal blackjack here."

"You have a house here. You could do something else."

It seems like years since I stood at my apartment window and looked over the parking lot, read the pink slip from the Golden Nugget.

"What did your mother think of your husband?"

I look at Tildy. She's smiling. It's amazing how her mind slips from one subject to another. Maybe she does have a screw loose.

"*Ex*-husband. And she died before I met him."

I met Bill one night with some people from work. We went to the Paris Hotel to eat at the buffet. The Paris is supposed to make visitors feel like they're in France. Bill was dealing blackjack. The man had great hands, a great body. As he was shuffling the cards, he looked at me, winked. Twenty minutes later on his break, he walked around the table and started talking, and that was the end of my life as I knew it. Before Bill, I paid the rent, the gas, the lights; after, my overdrawn checkbook tells the story.

We went out the next night and Bill told me he was deal-ing blackjack until he could get his computer company started. Claimed he had a degree in computer science. Right!

Three months later we were married. He charged things on my credit cards, didn't pay one goddamned bill, then split with everything I owned.

"What do you think she would have thought of your hus-band?" Tildy asks, smiles again.

"Who?"

"Your mama."

"She probably wouldn't." I look around the kitchen. "My mother didn't have much use for husbands."

CHAPTER 5

Magnolia Hall
April 1861

Mama made the trip out to visit day before yesterday. She fawned over the new house and my husband, claimed he is perfect for her daughter, then raised her eyebrow in that way she has, and I knew what she really meant. That I was spoiled and might not deserve the things I have.

She went on about the brightness of the rooms, the nice, new furniture. And, oh, she talked about the china, the silver tea set and the green brocade for settees James has brought back from Raleigh and Charleston. On and on she trilled!

"My daughter is so blessed to have all these possessions."

Mama loves pretty things. She always says that beautiful possessions make a house a home. She buys even though Father lectures her about spending so much money on furnishings. It is the one thing she does not listen to.

As she roamed the house, she talked about how impressed her friends were going to be when they saw the lovely home her daughter's husband had provided.

I asked when her friends would be arriving and Mama just smiled and informed me I should ready myself for them to call any day.

A married woman must be prepared for visitors any time, day or evening. Then she went on to tell me how fortunate I am. We stood in the hallway by the stairs, and she stopped for a moment, looked at me a long time then took my hand in hers. She bit her bottom lip until all the color was gone, then whispered,

"Do you love your husband, Charlotte? Tell Mama you are happy."

Her brown eyes looked so serious, I could not hurt her so I nodded, just once. The small lie seemed to make her feel better.

"I knew you would. Father always makes the right decisions. Now when my friends come to visit, show them everything, and be sure to act as happy as you are."

I'm not looking forward to visitors, yet I kept this a secret from Mama, too.

Suddenly Mama laughed and announced that soon, if I am a good wife, we will fill our home with babies and Mr. Alexander and I would be considered old married folk.

Children! Old married folk!

I still feel like such a child.

Yet I must confess I do think about James in a different way than the day I married him. In the past few weeks he has shown me kindness beyond what I expected from a husband. When he is home, he sits with me on the veranda in the evening, and we discuss the weather. Sometimes he compliments the evening meal. Lately, he has unpinned my hair, and his fingers comb through it, very delicately. I cannot say I like what he does, yet I do not mind it. James also talks of our children and how this house will be their refuge. He wants his sons to have something they can call their own when he is gone, when we both depart to heaven.

I smile at his melancholy. A woman of eighteen can hardly imagine not having her feet planted on the goodly North Carolina soil. I feel as if I will be here forever!

Oh, my heavens, I almost forgot. I do go on in my writing. During Mama's visit, she presented me with a large brown package. I untied the string and pulled the paper away. Mama is the one who loves to receive presents. I was so surprised she brought me one because she and Father had already given us a wedding gift.

While I was opening her package, she sighed so much I thought she might be fainting. Really, she is like a child on her birthday when there is a present. Underneath the paper lay a crystal compote Father purchased in New York City long ago. Even as a little girl, I admired the bowl, knew my mother cherished it. I never thought she'd give it away. After I thanked her properly, I vowed her gift will be cherished.

Some people might believe I am frivolous to think so highly of glass. But my thoughts are not of the cost, or the way the crystal catches the sparkle of the sun in the dining room. No, the gift represents something more, how Mama loves me, and how we are family.

After she left, Charity placed the gift in the mahogany china cabinet in the dining room and said she will dust it every day. What would I do without Charity? She is only a few years older than I. She came to live with us when I was born—to be my playmate. Mama tells me I need to be more severe with the servants. She never uses the word slave, but that is what Charity is. My parents have five servants. They treat them well and expect their children to do the same. But Father has instilled a severity in Mama that I hope to never cultivate.

I struggle every day to be firm and tell the servants what to do. I do not like bossing them, but I must. James is gone much of the time and expects me to run the household well.

Thankfully, I do not have to be Charity's master. She works so diligently. I would ask my husband to release her, but I know he will not. This, and many parts of him, his feelings about our servants, I do not understand.

In many ways he is kind. Yet he does not see the travesty in owning people like things—like crystal compotes and mahogany tables.

No one shall read these pages now!

While I write, Charity is singing. She loves to sing more than she cherishes breathing and she has a beautiful voice. She is tall, slender and dark, yet her face is coarse. She has told me her songs are her only freedom. A long time ago she confessed that when she sings, she goes to unknown places where she pretends to be free.

Once, I thought I might try to talk to my husband about the slaves, but I am too shy. And now there is too much trouble brewing to say a word. Some people have granted their servants freedom, but they are looked down upon and are called trouble starters.

Maybe women understand freedom more than men because no matter what our color, we are not free. We must listen to our husbands, our parents—unlike men, who take commands from no one. Before I married I claimed foolishly that no man would be "my lord and master" yet I did not know I would never be without someone to tell me what to do.

I fear for Charity and the other servants. Like me, they will never be their own guide or find a true home.

Magnolia Hall
Greensville, NC
June 2000

"Goodness, child, you don't have to pay me. Alexandria is finally out of school and I saved plenty. He helps me, too." Tildy points toward the ceiling then climbs down from the step stool she is perched on. Her face is covered with yellow paint flecks.

A few minutes ago I walked into the kitchen and found Tildy painting the wall by the sink. That's when I told her again she *cannot* work at Magnolia Hall for free, and since I don't have any money, she can't work here at all.

"I have money from my IRA. Plus if I take a wage from you, I'll lose my Social Security." She wipes her face, smears the tiny yellow specks, making them look like faraway meteors flying across a dark sky.

"Mr. Grey paid every one of my Social Security payments when he was in the chips. We'll just call my time at Magnolia Hall visits. You and me gonna be real friends."

"Tildy…" I stop. She's been here two days, and I've told her numerous times I'm not staying, but she won't believe me.

"You've got some paint on your face," I say instead.

"I'll get it off with alcohol. Don't you worry none." She finds a bottle under the sink, splashes some of the clear liquid on a rag she's found then hands it to me. "Give me a hand, please, honey."

I rub at the yellow dots, smear them more, but then like magic they disappear.

"I don't have any money, Tildy. It's best I stay with my plan, to sell, go home."

"Money's not important."

"It is when you don't have any and you need it. I charged my airline ticket. My bills are due. I can't find anyone to fix the wall." I spent half the day down at the Quick Stop phoning places to find someone to fix the upstairs wall. Not one person could come out to even give me an estimate.

Tildy starts up the step stool again.

"I can't let you bust your ass around here for free."

"Honey, don't cuss. And I like working." She turns from the step stool, opens the refrigerator, pulls out a full plate and sets it on the table. "Sit down and have some lunch. It'll calm you down."

I look at the plate and my stomach growls so loud Tildy hears.

"See there. I knew you were hungry." Tildy laughs, her head back, her eyes closed. "I'm getting to know you real good."

My stomach forces me to sit.

"You need me. And I need you. At least your stomach needs Tildy. But goodness, you shouldn't wait until you're starving."

I have to admit I'm eating better than ever. In Vegas my lunch consists of a yogurt and Diet Pepsi. And dinner, since Bill left, well, that's been frozen egg rolls and too much cheap rosé.

I pick up the fork and touch the red Jell-O. It jiggles.

Tildy leans close. The faint scent of alcohol surrounds me. "Go on now. Raspberry is the best flavor. I'm showering you in real Southern cooking. Your bones been aching for it, even though you didn't know. Why, your daddy was a Southerner through and through, despite the fact he didn't live here when he got older. Now things are changing."

Every time Tildy mentions my father I remember his face, young, smiling, and I swear I can almost hear his laugh. The memories are shadowy, like I'm looking through one of the sheer curtains in the living room—I want to see more, but I just can't manage it.

"I told you I don't remember much about him, about this house," I say, almost like an excuse.

"I'll show you some places where he might have taken you. Maybe that'll help."

"What's the point?"

"Honey, he was here, sat right where you are sitting and had his breakfast."

In California, my father always sat at the table in the kitchen. He'd lean over and touch my cheek with his little finger. Just touch it like there was a dot on my face he wanted to cover up. Then he'd laugh.

Tildy sits across from me.

"There's lots you could find out. Your daddy, when he was older and would visit, used to stand over by that sink and drink his coffee, talk a blue streak."

"I've spent a lot of time forgetting him and I'm fine with that."

"But he's your daddy. Don't you want to remember him?"

"Not really. After my parents were divorced, he never came around, never called. Why would I care now?"

"Don't you want to know who you come from, why he did something like that? He was a good man."

"How good could he have been if he just let my mother leave, take me, never wonder if I was okay?"

Tildy shakes her head. "That just doesn't seem like him."

"My only goal right now is to fix that wall, sell—"

"I think you should learn more about your daddy."

"I don't."

"But from what you've said, you don't have much to go back to."

"I don't have a job right now, but I'll find another one."

"If that's what's important to you."

"I don't need any more memories. Besides, it's too late. He's dead, I'm older."

"Now you're sounding like Mr. Grey. It's never too late."

"I'm satisfied with the way things are," I say, knowing it's a lie, and I wonder if Bill thought about how he was changing everything when he was packing up my things. Maybe he convinced himself everything would be all right, better. He was great at telling lies. His face, midwestern handsome, would get so serious when he told me how he'd struggled through college, how he was in love with me. Deep down did he believe all he said? Or just not care?

"His heart wanted to see you, you just gotta believe that."

I hear myself laugh, shake my head. "My father didn't try too hard. I was only three hundred miles away." I look around the strange kitchen, wonder what the hell I'm doing here listening to this foolishness.

"Honey, I don't know you as well as I should, but I can tell you're a fine young woman, and I'm sure your father thought so, too."

"Young? I'm almost forty-one, for God…goodness sakes."

"That's a baby. Eat your food," she says.

"Only if you'll eat with me and stop working. And if you promise that I can do the dishes."

"No way, Miss Juliette. If you broke a dish, why, Mr. Grey would never forgive me."

"I'll stick up for you. They're mine now."

She looks at me, and we both laugh.

"I think I will join you." She moves to the refrigerator, pulls out a bowl and platter and soon she's sitting beside me, the other blue-and-white plate in front of her, maybe the only other plate like it in the world.

"Mr. Grey is loving this, you and me having a meal together."

"Why do you talk about him in the present tense?" I ask around the chicken salad I've just shoved in my mouth.

"Why, he's alive as one of those trees or flowers out there." She points to the bedraggled backyard that needs mowing. "I know he still frets. People in heaven can worry just like us. I'm sure your daddy worries about you, wanting you to understand he's sorry for not seeing you enough."

"People worry in heaven? I thought that place was suppose to be worry-free." I have no idea what I'm talking about. I'm not religious. My mother never went to church, claiming there was nothing beyond this crappy life, and sometimes, I believe she's right.

"You're right! I bet Mr. Grey's happy and having a real good time knowing you're enjoying the family home. Now let's say our blessing."

Tildy's hand covers mine. She bows her head then looks up, catches me staring at her. "It's blessing time. Are you ready?"

I don't want to be rude, so I lower my eyes and she squeezes my hand.

"Dear Lord, bless our food, help Miss Juliette love Magnolia Hall and cherish all her memories here. Also help her find out about her father. Also bless my Alexandria, and good Lord, please bless me and keep me safe so I can help Miss Juliette. I would also like to see some grandchildren come my way—"

"Amen."

Tildy looks up, shakes her head then drops her chin.

"Sorry, I thought you were finished."

"And dear Lord, slow Miss Juliette down a little so she's

not so antsy. She needs to stop and smell the roses, not worry so much about money, and also could you really love Mr. Grey, Mr. James, the two Miss Charlottes and Miss Juliette's mother and keep them in your arms. Maybe you'd better make sure you don't get Mr. James and Miss Juliette's mother too close, you must know they didn't get along, as Miss Juliette says your heaven should be worry-free."

Tildy pauses as if to test her pull with God, and when I don't jump the gun she speaks.

"Amen." Then she lifts her gaze and smiles. "See. Praying works real fast. When we finish our meal, I've got something special to show you. I know you'll be interested. It's part of your family, part of you."

"Show me what?"

Her eyes light up. "Something special."

"I have to go back to the Quick Stop and get someone out here to fix that friggin' wall." I run my finger over the blue flowers lining the plate, feel bad for what I've just blurted out.

"Mighty pretty, isn't it? It's my favorite," Tildy says, and beams again. "Mr. Grey and me, we decided to keep two place settings of each set of china. Now I'm glad we did. This one's been in the family since the first Miss Charlotte moved here. Mr. Grey is so proud of it. Miss Charlotte, she loved her china, too. You just wait till you see what I have to show you. Honey, you're just gonna love it."

I put a tiny jewel of Jell-O in my mouth. Nod. It melts and I really can't understand what all the fuss is about. It tastes like colored water.

CHAPTER 6

Magnolia Hall
Greensville, NC
June 2000

I stack our two plates by the sink.

"Come on," Tildy says, and touches me on the shoulder.

"I'll wash the dishes first, won't take a minute." I really don't care if the dishes get done, I just don't want Tildy to do them. I feel guilty about all the work she's done. And deep down, I really don't want to know any more about the house, my uncle's belongings or what happened here.

"Plenty of time to do the dishes." Tildy stands with her hands on her hips.

"Tildy…" Her smile vanishes and I don't know how to tell her to leave me alone. I'm not good at telling people no, and that's pretty obvious with my life. "As long as it will take just a minute."

"Less than a minute." She guides me from the sink into the dining room, drags a chair to the far corner and climbs on it.

"What are you doing?" I go to where she is. "God, Tildy, you're going to kill yourself."

"I've done this a thousand times. Don't worry." She unloops a thick velvet cord. "Aren't these drapes the worst? We gave the good ones away. Heard some woman from Charlotte snatched them up two hours after I left, used them for a Victorian bed-and-breakfast. I didn't tell Mr. Grey, but I went down to the Salvation Army and got these to replace the others."

The drapes are faded beige.

"Thought having some drapes would make Mr. Grey feel better but, I declare, it made him feel worse. He turned up his nose, said the family ones should be here. I told him these could become the family ones."

Tildy straightens the drapes, takes hold of the cord and pulls. "Here we go."

Warm air moves above my head and I look up. The carved mahogany wood over the table is moving back and forth, stirring the air.

"It's a fan. God, I thought it was just a decoration."

"Decoration, nothing! It's a punkah that freshens the air." Tildy tugs on the velvet cord again, huffing, her butt dipping toward the wall. "I hid the cord so Mr. Grey wouldn't sell the punkah. Out of sight, out of mind, you know what I mean? He didn't come in this room too much after he started giving things away. At the beginning it was all about these ugly old drapes, then he wasn't strong enough to worry about them. I like coming in here. When I touch this cord I feel so close to my family—like my ancestors are with me right now."

"Really? You believe in spirits?" My heart races a little at her weirdness.

"Goodness, no! I feel a closeness. I pretend I can hear them telling me to be strong. Don't worry, we'll survive, no matter what! My great-great-grandmama pulled this same cord just like this, while the family was dining." She pulls the cord harder and the fan moves faster.

More air swirls around me, and when I think about Tildy's family working here I feel a little dizzy. I close my eyes and swallow.

"What's the matter, Miss Juliette?"

"I can't watch you do that." My stomach has tightened to iron and a warmth inches its way up my throat. The fan thunks to a stop and suddenly she's beside me, her arm around my waist. Her body is warm, sweaty, and the close- ness of her hugging makes me pull back.

"Oh, child. You look so upset?" Her crossed arms press her breasts down.

"The slave thing. How can you stay here?"

"I like being where my family was. Besides—" Tildy points to the table surface as if she's distracting a child "—Magnolia Hall is beautiful. Look at the shine on this table. It catches the sunlight in such a beautiful way." Her hand flutters just above the surface.

I glance down at our faces side-by-side—a faint mirror of wavy images.

"Isn't this table wonderful?" Her fingers lightly touch my reflected cheek and then her own. "Look how pretty."

I stare at Tildy's reflection. "But doesn't it bother you, knowing what your relatives went through here?"

She smiles, then looks away. "It used to. Mr. Grey loved to have dinner here." She points to the captain's chair. "He told me the first Miss Charlotte had a great fondness for this table. I talked him out of selling it time after time. I slipped money in his checking account without him knowing. He was pretty sick at the end, didn't know. Selling the dining-room table would have been the end of him, but keeping it didn't keep him around, either. He was so mad he was sick, like he couldn't bear to leave Magnolia Hall."

I think about my mother, how when she found out she had liver cancer she wouldn't talk to me for three weeks, lay in bed facing the wall. She was angry at her world—and part of that world was me.

"So he never accepted he was dying?" I ask so I don't have to think about my mother lying among moist, twisted blue sheets.

"No. I don't think he wanted to leave this beautiful house."

I face her, have to ask. "Tildy, your relatives were slaves here. Doesn't it bother you to think about that? To be here, remember what happened? How they must have been treated?"

"I quit Magnolia Hall in the sixties. Didn't come back for five months. I had an Afro, big, too." Her hands pat at imaginary bouffant hair around her head. "I could have hidden my entire IRA in that hairdo."

"You left? Why'd you come back?"

"I missed the way I got to watch the light come through these dining-room windows every afternoon—the same light my family watched. Can you imagine that? Me seeing the same light? They kept this place going. I couldn't leave them behind. I went to work at the Hilton up on I-Forty and College as a housekeeper. Mr. Grey came in one day, asked me to come back, told me he'd give me a raise, increase my health insurance. Only had to work three days for five days' pay. Who's gonna pass that up? I felt sorry for him. The man looked lost. Told me no one knew how to take care of Magnolia Hall like I did. I finally got him to admit he missed me."

"Did he miss you or need help?"

Tildy stiffens, cranes her neck a little. "He missed me, believe me."

"I'm not black, but—"

"I wouldn't have known that if you hadn't told me." She laughs, touches my hand.

"What I mean is I don't know how you can stand coming here. You must think about what your relatives went through."

"I do. But I grew up knowing this place. Mr. Grey, he paid me well all those years. And he only had me pull the cord on Saturdays when he ate dinner."

"What an asshole."

"Miss Juliette, lighten up, I'm kidding. He didn't do that."

"I can't find anything funny right now in what we're talking about."

Tildy pats my shoulder. "You and I are gonna become real friends. We don't have to be so serious all the time. Don't you understand, it wouldn't have made sense for me to get mad and leave Magnolia Hall. Mr. Grey was funding my IRA. I had a great retirement program. Better than those people at the Hilton. And my people's memories are here.

Where was I going to get another job that had early retirement?"

I nod, she's right about that. "But still—"

"You know, Mr. Grey had some writings of the first Miss Charlotte. He told me Miss Charlotte wrote about taking care of my great-great-grandmother when she had her baby."

"Writings—where are they?"

"Don't know. Mr. Grey must have gotten rid of them, like all the other things."

"Then how do you know what he told you was true?" My stomach is tying in another hard knot. Why the hell am I asking this? I've never been a person who stood up for anything. I've barely crawled through life, for God's sake, with all my man problems, marriage problems, money problems.

"Of course what he told me is true. He was an honest man. Now you'll carry on the stories, the family."

"Tildy, people lie, and I'm not staying, and that's the truth."

"Magnolia Hall will give you something, just wait and see." Her ebony lashes are thick and so curly they seem to grow back into themselves.

"This is just a house."

She nods as if she understands what I'm saying. "If you

keep Magnolia Hall you'll have a nice home when you decide to have a family."

"Family! At my age?" But my chest starts to ache with her suggestion. Sometimes there's a little part of me that feels like a bruised peach—one that's been put back in the pile too many times.

"You've got to keep yourself open for anything, Miss Juliette. Don't close up. Even magnolia blossoms open when the sun hits them just right."

She steps in the square of sunlight from the window, lifts her chin, closes her eyes and raises her arms as if she's worshipping some god I don't know about.

"I've been divorced three times. No more romance for me. You can have it." I step in the opposite window's light—dazzling.

"All I'm saying is now that you have the house, it would be nice if you had someone to care about you."

"I like where I am." I think about my crappy Las Vegas apartment, the smoky, clanging casinos. The desert heat, the traffic. "Well, some things I don't like, but I live there. It's comfortable."

"I love to dream." Tildy smiles, waves her hands. "You should, too."

"Dreams are for suckers," I say, and walk back into the kitchen.

Magnolia Hall
April 1861

I am thankful Mama allowed me to bring Charity to Magnolia Hall. In the evenings, if Mr. Alexander is away, we work on our sewing in the parlor.

I know I shouldn't, but I allow Charity to sit in the parlor with me. When we were little and played together, we would hide in the attic, high above everyone, and pray no one would find us. We laughed and sang and once she told me how she missed her mother, but she could not remember what she looked like. And once she told me how she wanted to be free.

Even then I knew Father would never approve of such talk, so I shushed her, swatted at her hand then went downstairs, leaving her there.

We were so young then.

Now, when my husband is gone, I am free to say and think things I normally would not.

The other day I told Charity I missed living in Greensville. She stared at me, didn't say a word. Suddenly, she asked what I thought her mama might look like. She was taken from her family when she was two and sold to the highest bidder—my father. He bought her as a playmate for me. When I was a little girl, I thought of her as a doll, and I would dress her, make her sit in corners.

This is not the first time she asked me about her mama. But this time I made up a story. I guess because I miss my family so much. I dressed her mama in an imaginary green velvet cloak, gave her the shiniest black hair and made her walk like a princess. I cannot imagine not knowing my own family—where I came from. But many of the servants know nothing of their background. Maybe that is why I keep my diary, so when I have my own family they will know who they are.

For the past few days, Charity and I have placed all the new furniture the best we know how. Then in the afternoons, she sings and rubs the surfaces with the beeswax Mr. Alexander brought back from Raleigh. A few mornings ago I found Charity in the dining room polishing the mahogany tabletop. She startled, then when she saw it was me she smiled, brought me to the edge of the dining table. The draperies were open and sunshine was gushing through the windows, painting the room with a delightful brilliance.

"Look, Miss Charlotte, there's something special right here on this dining table."

She pointed to the gleaming surface. I stepped closer and looked down. There was my face reflected back. Charity leaned closer.

"Don't you look beautiful?"

I laughed, told her she was being too nice.

Then Mr. Alexander called. We both jumped at his voice. Charity picked up her polishing rag and began rubbing the table.

My husband walked into the dining room and declared he would have the roof fixed immediately. I had forgotten about the rain seeping in the bedroom.

"I have prayed the fine magnolia paper from Raleigh will not be ruined," I said softly.

Mr. Alexander instructed me not to worry about such matters.

"Charity, sing to Miss Charlotte at night to soothe her."

I did not tell him she has been singing to me since she was small. He does not like to be corrected. The Divine Providence gifted Charity with the voice of an angel. And me—the voice of a duck.

As he spoke, Charity stared at the dining-room carpet, nodding.

"Yes, masser, I rightly will sing to Miss Charlotte."

Charity sings such beautiful songs. She pretends her mama taught them to her. Whenever she speaks of her mama, I see the familiar sadness in her eyes. Before I married I did not fully understand Charity's mood. I did not realize what it might be like to be without family. Now I do.

Mr. Alexander again turned to me, complimented the shine on the table. Suddenly, to my great surprise, he insisted I give his house a name. Before I could express my doubt that I should have this honor, he was gone. I gasped, and ran through the dining room, down the hall into the library, and suggested he should be the one to name his house.

He scolded me, and to my great surprise I stamped my foot. Instead of raising his voice, Mr. Alexander stepped to me, cradled my face in his hands and brought my gaze to his.

"Why are you out of sorts?"

I could feel the warmth of his hands on my face, and I confessed I was not worthy of choosing a name because I did not want to live here when we first wed. His eyes turned dull for a moment. Then he laughed and ordered me, as the lady of the house, to find a proper name.

That night as Charity sang, I fretted. She told me if she could name the house she would call it Magnolia because of the beautiful trees surrounding us. The word touched something in me and sprang to life.

Again, I galloped, very unladylike, to the library.

"I have picked Magnolia."

Mr. Alexander put down his book and gazed at me as if he were trying to look at the sun at noon. Then he laughed.

"You have been out cutting flowers?"

I grew a little faint, out of breath, explained myself, then said we might add "hall" so visitors would not look for a flower or tree when they come to visit.

Mr. Alexander laughed again, claimed I was very talented in the art of naming houses.

And now, days later, I do feel closer to the house. You see, yesterday I went out beyond the veranda and studied a magnolia tree. They are sturdy. I held one of the lovely delicate moonlit flowers in my hands as if it were a baby. If the Divine Providence blesses me with children, they will be strong—my beautiful white flowers.

Yet my happiness was spoiled soon after.

Mr. Alexander has begun to talk of the trouble brewing everywhere. His disposition worries me, and last night my happiness was dashed to the ground—broken into pieces like the blue flowered dish I dropped when he mentioned war. He declares he will fight if there is war.

Later, when we sat on the veranda, the sunset turned us into light shadows, and evening provided a veil for my questions. First I mentioned my head ached from all the talk of war. James sat beside me and held my hand. The blood rushed to my skin, and he laughed and told me I was married and did not need to blush. He undid my hair and combed his fingers through the strands, tenderly rubbing my scalp until my headache was all but gone.

By then I did not want to talk of the trouble brewing, so I mentioned the house. James went on about what a beauty our home has turned into. I thanked him again for the rocker he brought back from Raleigh. It has a beautiful yellow pineapple painted on the back.

He smiled, stood and brought me to my feet.

And I said a little prayer before he led me through the front door and up the stairs.

"God, grant grace and peace to our home."

CHAPTER 7

Magnolia Hall
Greensville, N.C.
June 2000

I'm standing in the middle of the library thinking about my father. I should be looking for someone to fix the upstairs, but after Tildy and I talked in the dining room, I wandered into the library again.

When I was seven I decided my father was dead. One day in Mrs. Churnick's second-grade class the other girls were talking about how strong their fathers were. After they finished, I said my father was dead, then I spelled the word slowly, *d-e-a-d*. Mrs. Churnick turned around, looked at me sympathetically, patted my head, and some of the kids stared like I'd been somewhere they would never go.

I tasted true power that day.

Three days later, I climbed in my mother's '62 blue Chevy

Impala, next to her. She smelled like roses in the morning, before she went to work at the Fremont Hotel as a hostess in the coffee shop. Her gold hair lay against her shoulders, and for a moment she looked unreal.

"My dad's dead, *d-e-a-d*," I said, hoping she would pat me on the head.

My mother turned, looked at me for a moment, as if I were a stranger who had crawled in uninvited. And then she slapped my face. My skin stung and the blow forced all the air out of my chest. I couldn't cry, couldn't do anything but gasp for a happier life.

She sat there, staring straight ahead, her fingers gripping the dull blue opaque steering wheel.

I finally caught my breath and began crying. She turned again, her haunting, sad expression crowding me against the door.

"You can't go to school now. Look at your face."

I touched my tingling skin, wet, and felt the shame of not knowing what I said wrong, wondering why she didn't like me.

My mother got out of the car, leaned in through the open window. I could see the glistening sweat on her forehead and above her lip. "Your father is not dead. And I'm sorry."

For years I wondered if she was sorry because he wasn't dead or if she felt bad that she slapped me—she never said. It was a secret she kept from me, and maybe herself.

I look around the library, stare at the old rocking chair in the middle of the room. Sunlight cascades through the windows. Something clatters in the kitchen—Tildy and her constant doings. Yet, I know I'd be very lonely if she weren't here.

I sit in the old rocking chair, rub the arm. The wood is incredibly smooth.

Magnolia Hall
May 1861

I should feel blessed by the Divine Providence, yet I am afraid. And to make matters worse, because I was bursting with news, I have made Charity my confidante and sworn her not to tell a soul!

I believe I am with child!

If Mama knew, she would insist I move back to Hemsley because James is away so many days now. I do not want to leave here, as Magnolia Hall has become my home.

Mama would surely claim I am the most foolish girl she knows. First, I did not want to leave Hemsley, go to my husband's home, and now I do not want to come back!

And I do not understand my feelings, either.

A week ago when I realized I might be with child, I

knew in my heart I must make Magnolia Hall a place for him or her.

Yesterday, I told Charity I feel frightened even though I know birthing is a woman's duty, something we must do. Charity smiled and told me not to be afraid because I am in the hands of the angels now. She also pledged she would stay by my side and help me. She took it upon herself to move the pineapple rocking chair into the library, and in the evenings I sit beside James as he reads. Just weeks ago he was a stranger to me—yet now we are connected by a child.

Last night he looked very handsome with the firelight dancing on his face. I wondered if the baby will have his fine almond-shaped blue eyes or straight nose? Everything belongs to James, and so will this baby. Possessions seem to mean so much to him—like Mama.

The last time he returned from Charleston, he brought more drapery material and new chairs for the parlor. I told him I was very grateful, however, we do not need another item for the house. I am beginning to realize silver and mahogany do not make a home. A soft touch and laughter create a place for one to feel safe. Two nights ago I boldly asked James if he thought the silver teapot or the pineapple rocking chair would keep us safe and protected.

He only laughed, told me I think too much.

This morning in the parlor, I told Charity I feel different. She looked at me, tilted her head as if by doing so she could see my changes. How can she understand? She is much like a child herself. I explained that I must make sure the walls and floors overflow with goodness.

Charity nodded, yet her expression questioned me. She must think me very strange at times.

Magnolia Hall
Greensville, NC
June 2000

Tildy's tennis shoes squeak against the wooden floor.

"Miss Juliette?"

I open my eyes, focus on the ceiling.

"Miss Juliette?"

I inch the yellow blanket over my head, take a tired breath. The sheets smell like bleach and sun. I'm used to sleeping till ten. I've always worked day shift in Vegas, twelve to eight. Last night I went to bed at eleven, but I didn't sleep very well. I woke up at one, started thinking about the stupid wall I can't seem to get anyone to fix.

"Miss Juliette?"

I try not to sigh but I do, and slip the blanket just below my eyes, look at the squares of morning light on the flowered walls.

"Miss Juliette?" Tildy stands at the foot of the bed. "You awake?"

"I am now."

"Oh, my goodness, I didn't mean to wake you. But you'd better rise and shine, Miss Juliette. Rise and shine 'cause it's almost noon."

"How close to noon?"

"Why, it's already eight. Closer to noon than midnight. And there's a beautiful North Carolina morning just waiting for you."

"I didn't sleep well." I groan and pull the covers over my head again. She tugs at it gently, moves it from my face.

"You aren't worrying about that old wall, are you? Come on, honey, get up. You'll feel better when you call some people to fix it. Plus, didn't you say you should get back in touch with the attorney?"

I ease up on my elbow, groan again. She's right. I need to make phone calls, get an appointment to see Ron, find out if there is any extra money to help fix the house.

"Are you sick?" she asks.

"No. Just tired."

"Oh."

I sit up more. "I'm fine, really." I yawn and she does, too.

"Why aren't you sleeping at night? Mr. Grey, why he slept like a baby."

"Strange place, I guess."

"It's natural you'd be affected. The walls in this house are filled with memories."

"Maybe it's the mildew." I laugh but she doesn't.

"Miss Juliette, you're gonna be fine. Mildew never hurt anyone. Coffee's ready. I'll bring you a cup. Or would you rather have tea this fine morning?"

"Tildy, you don't have to do any of this! I'm not paying you. And you've done too much already." I throw back the covers. "In fact, I'll get out of bed and you get in, then I'll bring you coffee, or would you rather have tea?"

Tildy laughs. "Miss Juliette, you are funny. I don't mind. I want to make you feel at home so you'll stay."

"Tildy...I'm..." I stop myself. I've said this too many times.

"You'll be comfortable soon. Everything takes time, believe me."

I look at her. Her expression is so serious. "I appreciate everything you're doing for me, really I do." I get out of bed.

"You need to do what you need to do. That's what Mr. Grey always used to say. Yesterday I looked in from the kitchen and watched you rocking in Miss Charlotte's pineapple chair. You were rubbing the arm just like Mr. Grey used to do. Everyone who's lived here has rocked in that chair. Why, I've taken a few trips in her myself. You should have seen yourself, so relaxed, no wrinkles on your forehead, like now, took ten years off your face."

"Well then, glue my butt to that seat."

"How you talk, Miss Juliette!"

I grab my jeans, a T-shirt. "I'll just put these on," I say, and start for the bathroom.

"Your grandmother used to buy me clothes. Dressed me up like a doll baby."

I turn, look at Tildy, who's smiling. Her fingers are resting on her chin. She's sitting on the edge of the bed.

"She did?"

"Sure. I was the best-dressed girl in the state. Mr. Grey's mama was a good woman, like you are, full of affection, loving and sweet, too."

"That's definitely not me."

"You are, but you don't know it. From what I can tell you had a hard time of it. I never noticed it before, but I'm beginning to see you don't know who you are, do you?"

"Like anyone does?"

"Some people do. When you do, you might meet—"

"Oh, no. I'm not meeting anyone, Tildy. As I said, I've been married three crappy times."

"You haven't found the right man, someone to appreciate you."

"I pick the wrong people."

"How old were you when you got married?"

"Which time?"

"All of them."

"The first time I was eighteen. It seemed like the right thing to do. We didn't know what marriage was. All I wanted was out of the house, away from my mother, so I got married. How smart is that?"

"That's about how old I was, too."

"You've been married?"

"I got Alexandria, don't I?"

"You don't have to be married for that."

"In my day it was best if you were."

"Who is he?"

"An army man, going off to war. We had four good weeks."

"Four weeks, that's all?" My heart jumps a little, thinking about Tildy having someone and then losing him so quickly.

"Yes, but they were the best weeks of my life."

"And you never married again?"

"Only man for me was Johnny Butler. I never wanted anyone else. I've got all the sweet good memories."

"You married once, me married over and over again. Life is weird."

"I loved him. No one like him in the world."

"How'd you know he was the right one?"

"There are times a person just knows. You know?"

"No. I don't get vibes, have intuition."

"I'm not talking about any old voodoo. I'm talking about a feeling that's just right. Then you make a family."

"Tildy…I'm not like that. I don't even think about my family." I listen to what I'm saying, know it's not the truth, at least it isn't now that I've come here.

"You don't?"

"Well, I've been thinking about my father and mother more. It's just because I'm here and you've been talking about them."

"Why'd you marry the second time?" she asks.

"I was twenty-five, still not very smart. He seemed like a nice guy."

"You didn't love him?"

"I thought I did, but I guess I didn't. The love kind of stopped when I caught him with another woman."

Tildy scrunches her nose—like she can't believe what I've just said. "And what about the last one, the one who took all your money?"

"I didn't have very much. I have very bad judgment when it comes to men. Tildy, haven't you dated anyone else?"

"Goodness, no!"

"Why not? How old are you?"

"Old enough to know better than to tell anyone."

"But you've been alone a long time. There must have been someone you were interested in."

Tildy's eyes widen, and her lips pull into a thin line. "I have my memories of Johnny. That's all I need."

"Weren't you lonely? Aren't you lonely now?"

"No. I have this house, my child and now you."

"But Tildy—"

"This is all I need."

And for an insane moment, and I've experienced a few since I've been here, I want to feel like she does.

"I know you believe me." She smiles. "I'll get your coffee."

"Let me shower and come downstairs."

"Whatever you say. I've got something special to show you, if you are willing. How about it?"

"You showed me something special yesterday."

"There's a few more things."

"Really?"

She nods.

Oh, God.

"What I want to show you won't take but a minute. You can make your calls after. We're going to the attic."

I wonder if she's serious. "Attic? What attic?"

"Why, honey, there's a door in the closet down at the end of the hall. That inspector didn't find it?"

"No, thank God." I think about the damage that might be up there.

"He probably overlooked it. Had too much on his mind."

"What's in the attic?"

"Something I managed to save." Tildy pushes herself off the bed and her tennis shoes squeak against the wood. "You hurry with your bath, and when you finish, I'll have your breakfast ready."

"Please…don't cook…." But my words, one by one, fall against the magnolia wallpaper.

Magnolia Hall
August 1861

My husband tries to hide his pride, yet the elation in his eyes is evident. He is jubilant I am having his child. When we sit on the veranda, he stares at me. I try to ignore his actions, but he makes it almost impossible.

I wish I could be as happy as he. I am frightened at the thought of growing huge, of having to push this child out of me. And then? I have never had to take care of little ones, so how will I know how to tend a baby?

Charity told me it is natural to take care of a child.

She said I will be fine, yet I cannot be sure. I have known women in town who have died from childbirth.

"Women are for babies and babies for women," Charity said.

The first time she said that I scolded her and told her I did not want her to mention my "situation." She held her hand to her hateful lips to hide a smile. I was so angry I wanted to slap her. Instead I stomped upstairs and stared at the wallpaper until the clock chimed on the half hour. Suddenly I burst into tears. Not a moment later, Charity was standing in front of me, claiming she was sorry and everything was going to be fine.

Imagine! Charity comforting me. Mama would be so disgraced if she knew what went on in James Alexander's house.

Last night I asked James if we are blessed with a boy may I call him Grey after my father. He smiled and agreed.

"Grey is a perfect name, a strong name and a fine way to honor your father and North Carolina."

I am sure he agreed so quickly because he is troubled that the doctor warned me about worrisome thoughts. I am to think only about pleasant things. He suggested I sing because some believe that music makes strong, happy babies. James demands I stop singing and find Charity to finish any of the songs I start. And she does with exuberance. She trills until her voice is hoarse.

With the terrible war, James is insisting I become more firm and strict with the servants. I am working to be forceful with Charity, yet I find it more and more difficult. When I am ready to reprimand her for a minor offense, which is all she ever commits, she looks at me with her brown eyes, and I only see goodness. Then she smiles and I cannot scold her or put her out.

Mama has told me the same. A week ago she came to Magnolia Hall. The first evening she reminded me I am too familiar with my servants and I should remain reserved. I explained I cannot be hateful to Charity since she soothes me so. Mama shook her head.

"A baby having a baby. Poor James Alexander, to be strapped with this."

I did not tell her that my feelings have changed for James, too. How would I explain the transition? At night when James and I are in bed and he is whispering to me, I cannot think of being anywhere but with him. Although I am still not sure what love is, my heart is softer now. In the early morning hours when I cannot sleep, I wonder if Mama feels the same about Father. Then my skin feels hot. I push the thoughts away and force myself to think of something proper like my Bible.

One morning when I was very tired, I asked Charity if she knew about love or thought about someone in a special way. She stared at the floor, shook her head hard. I should not confide in her, yet lately when a question comes into my mind, it spills out like water from a tipped bucket.

"Don't you care for someone?" I asked.

Her face began to pinch and grow small, and she shook her head more violently. I still have no idea if Charity knows about love between a man and woman.

At night when I am alone in our bed and the house is filled with moonlight, I rise, walk through each room and touch the walls. I lay my hands flat against the cool surfaces and think of James, and his baby inside me.

I have learned one must be patient and wait for what is true. I never thought these feelings would find me. My heart will always be grateful.

CHAPTER 8

Magnolia Hall
Greensville, NC
June 2000

"Did you find anyone?" Tildy asks as I walk into the kitchen. She's standing in front of the stove stirring something, her hips swaying.

"No. The people I call just laugh. I did get someone to promise they'd come out in four weeks." I sit at the table and rub my sweaty face.

"That's good."

"Tildy! I need to get home. I have to find a job, pay my rent or I'm going to get evicted."

She turns, smiles. "Four weeks might go by real fast."

"My rent is due in two. I'll be homeless."

"You've got Magnolia Hall."

I laugh at the absurdity. "Right. I forgot."

"What's next?" she asks.

"I'm going to call the attorney and find out if Grey had any money left."

"I can tell you there wasn't one red cent. At the end I was buying the groceries. The diapers."

"Diapers?"

"He ended up incontinent. Poor man. He was always so proud. Then to have that happen. Oh, good Lord above."

I think about my mother. How when I went to Desert Springs Hospice to her room while they were changing her, my eyes were drawn automatically to the dark blond mound of pubic hair rising up between her hipbones.

"So?" Tildy asks.

My thoughts swim among my mother's memory for a moment too long.

"Tildy, maybe there was some money that you don't know about, a small bank account somewhere?"

"Maybe. You gotta dream."

My arms feel cool and I shiver.

"You okay?"

"Fine. Maybe the attorney can float me a loan until I sell the house."

"You should rest for a while. Heat and humidity are hard on people."

"I can't." I push the chair back, stand, pick up my purse,

go out the door. Before I climb into the car that's like a small boat, I look back. Tildy is standing on the top step, watching me.

"I won't be long, really."

"There's no money, believe me. And what about what I was going to show you? You'll like it."

"I have to ask him."

I get in the car, back out. It's hot, muggy, and even though I've had a shower, I feel sticky. I drive down the tree-lined streets to the Quick Stop. Of course the phone is on the outside of the building, in the sun. I dig through my purse, find Ron's card, unbend the corners, pull two quarters out of my wallet and drop them in the slot. The receiver feels slick, and I wonder how many down-and-out desperate people have stood where I'm standing, thinking they're going to solve their problems with fifty cents.

The phone rings twice. I tell the voice on the other end who I am, ask to speak with Mr. Tanner. A moment later he's on the phone. His calm voice aggravates me.

"I need some help!"

"With what?"

"What do you think? The house. It didn't pass inspection. The upstairs wall has to be torn down, put back up. I can't find anyone to do it, and even if I could, I don't have any money to pay anyone. My uncle's housekeeper told me there's no money, but there has to be something left."

He doesn't say anything.

"Well?"

"She's right, there isn't any money. Just the house, the car. I've checked. In fact he still owes the doctor fifteen hundred dollars."

I'm dripping sweat. "Fifteen hundred dollars! I can't pay that! What the hell am I supposed to do?"

"I'll call the doctor, tell them you'll settle after you sell the house."

"That's the problem—I can't sell the damn house until I get the wall fixed, and I can't find anyone who can fix the wall, and even if I could, I won't be able to pay for it, so I can't sell the damn house." My words ring in my head, and I close my eyes. "Sorry, it's hot out here."

"Out where?"

"The phone at the house is off. I'm at the Quick Stop down the street."

"I had my secretary arrange to turn the power on. I forgot about the phone. I'll have her do that as soon as she can."

I imagine Ron sitting at a large amber desk, suit coat on, the air-conditioning in his office running full blast, and this makes me angrier.

"Ms. Carlton, are you still there?"

"Yes. I can't afford the phone." I feel like an idiot for calling. What the hell is this guy supposed to do about my problems? It's not his fault I got canned, married a dipshit, my uncle didn't take care of his house, left me the place because he forgot to make a will.

I realize Ron's talking and I've missed part of what he said. "I'm sorry."

"What are you sorry about?"

"I didn't hear what you said." I squint, look into the parking lot, watch a man climb into his pickup then stare at me. "I'm right in the sun. Is it always this humid?"

"Yes. Sometimes more so."

"Great."

A big drop of sweat plops on the sidewalk and I watch it darken the concrete.

"How much is the wall going to cost?" Ron asks.

"The inspector said about eight hundred dollars. But it doesn't matter because I can't get anyone to come out and give me an estimate. What the hell is going on in this town?"

"Expansion. You have to take the entire wall down?"

"Most of it, I guess. I really don't have a whole lot of construction experience."

I hear him laugh, and even though I'm angry, it's a nice sound.

"You wouldn't happen to know of anyone who could fix the bedroom wall? I don't know why I called you, but you're the only person I know in town besides Tildy and—"

"It's okay you called. I don't know anyone who can repair it. I could take a look at it."

"No, no really—"

"I did some remodeling work around my house—"

I feel desperate. "Well, if you have the time."

"The probate papers, they need to be signed, so I could come out."

"Oh, the papers," I hear myself say. "I forgot about them."

"I don't have any time today, but I could come by this evening at seven."

"Seven, tonight?"

"Yeah."

I nod, feel more sweat bead.

We decide he'll stop by then. I hang up, go into the store and buy the largest Coke I can find, the real stuff, not diet. I drink half before I pay for it. My lips and tongue feel sticky. I throw the rest in the trash and drive home.

Tildy is still in the kitchen. "Well?"

"There's no money."

"Should have listened to me. I'll lend you the money to get the wall fixed."

We are standing across from each other, she at the

sink, me by the table. I want to say yes, yes, yes, but I don't.

"No, I can't. You've done enough already."

"Haven't done nothing I don't want to do. You can pay me back."

"I'm already in debt up to my ass…sorry. I have a lot of bills. The lawyer's coming out tonight to have me sign probate papers and he's going to look at the wall."

"There's always somebody. Things will work out. Sit. I made you a meal. You need your strength. We're going to the attic in a bit."

I sit at the table, but I wish I hadn't agreed to go up to the attic. What's the point?

"I fixed you my best scrambled eggs, two biscuits with real butter, spiced peaches. Kind of like a brunch."

I look at the full plate Tildy has placed in front of me. "I feel like a baby bird with its mouth continuously open. I'll have to be rolled out of this house if I keep eating like this."

"'Bout time someone fed you, loved you a little. That's what kitchens are for." She smiles, looks around the kitchen. "This room was added on years ago. The original was a small building in back of the main house that had to be torn down. Your daddy loved this room."

I glance around, think about my father being here.

"Now eat your breakfast. You need the vitamins."

I pat my stomach. "My shorts are tight."

"People worry too much about their weight. Just this once you can clog your arteries. I decided we need to celebrate."

"Celebrate? What's to celebrate?"

"Magnolia Hall might be getting her wall fixed. Things are changing. There's plenty to celebrate. We both are healthy, life is good! Every morning I wake up happy to be alive, then when I get here I look out the kitchen window and say, *hallelujah!*"

She does a little mambo, holding a wooden spoon above her head.

"Maybe you ought to save the dancing for when the repairs actually take place."

"Great things already happened."

I laugh, feel good despite everything. "Why don't you eat, too?"

She smiles and I *really, really* like her.

"Well, I already ate, but a little more coffee and a biscuit or two might be nice. I should have made some gravy."

Tildy goes to the stove, brings back the old type percolator, the one with the glass ball on top, and pours coffee into the two cups already on the table. Steam rises up in ribbons. I sip mine and then fork eggs into my mouth. "Good."

"See what food can do. You know, honey, you might think about fixing the wall yourself."

"Me? Right! I have trouble pounding a nail to hang a picture."

"You could learn. We could go to Home Depot, look around."

I stop eating. "You think I could find a way to fix the wall at Home Depot?"

"Sure, they got everything. I'll help you. Now eat. If you gonna do all that work, then you need your strength. You don't eat much, do you?"

"Sometimes I forget to eat altogether. I get busy, and living alone, well, you should know."

"I always take care of myself. It's a new day, honey, and you're going to have it all." She stirs her coffee with the other silver spoon. "For dinner I'm planning something special. A roast just the way Mr. Grey used to like it. Pecans and pineapples. Mandarin orange Jell-O salad, candied carrots, pickled beets, a few more biscuits and sweet tea. Should hold you for a while."

"That'll hold me for a year."

"You like my cooking, don't you?"

"Who wouldn't?"

"What would you do if I didn't cook? Order that Chinese? That's no way for a body to survive. Slathering your insides with MSG. My land, you're nothing but a reed now. You could use a little fattening up. Diet when you go back to that dried-up Nevada."

"So you do understand I am going back?"

"I'm talking cooking. Nothing else."

"Tomorrow I'll take kitchen duty. I'll cook for you."

"Oh dear Lord!"

I laugh. "I can cook a little. Have some faith."

"It's not that. We forgot to say our prayers."

Tildy grabs my left hand and bows her head. A moment later she's looking at me. "You cook?"

"No, but I nuke a mean Lean Cuisine."

"Let's just leave it like it is. Me cooking and cleaning and you fixing up the house."

"I haven't done anything."

"You will. Did you cook for your husband?"

"Ex-husband."

"Did you?"

"He gambled, and gamblers stay in casinos."

"Where is he now?"

"Don't know, but wherever he is, he has all our furniture, if he didn't sell it, which he probably did." I think about the empty rooms I found, like Magnolia Hall's. My stomach tightens.

"He won't have a good life."

"Who?"

"Your ex."

"How do you know?"

"Because a person can't go living in lies and get anything back." Tildy reaches over and pushes my plate closer. "Eat, honey. Forget all those sad times. You'll be fine. Hard times are good for us."

"I don't think so."

"You're bitter, but you'll see." Her hand goes up and her index finger draws a small circle in the air. "Everybody should have fun. And you need it more than most."

"No time for fun. I'm fortysomething, and I don't even own a decent couch."

"Lord, child, there's a lot of couches in this world. Sounds like your husband was a professional bastard."

"Tildy!" But she's nailed Bill.

"The first time I laid eyes on you in this kitchen I knew you were as dry as a desert. I'm not talking about sex now. You need to find yourself a friend. Someone who wants to understand, who you'll let in."

"I don't need anyone to make me happy. I make myself happy." I touch my chest, as if to remind myself of some stupid women's magazine mantra.

"Everybody needs somebody."

"I'm over forty—it's too late. I lied to myself about trusting Bill, talked myself into thinking he was okay!"

"Don't give up. My mama used to say that the sun don't shine on one dog's butt all the time."

"Tildy!"

We both burst out laughing.

"It's true. Good luck rolls around. Just once in this house there wasn't love and that was a terrible time. The sun wasn't shining on anyone living here."

"When Grey died?"

"No, Mr. Grey dying was supposed to be, that's the nature of things. It was a long time ago." She takes a sip of coffee.

"What happened?"

"The war. Miss Charlotte wrote about the war in her diary. But Mr. Grey packed up all the memories and got rid of them. But this house, these walls still know."

"You don't believe that?" I like Tildy, but she acts so weird sometimes.

"A month ago, did you believe you'd own this house?"

I shake my head.

"That proves it. Things happen we don't understand."

Magnolia Hall
September 1861

Mama sent a note by messenger saying everyone at Hemsley is ill with influenza. She begged me to send

Charity to Greensville to help out. I hate to let her go, but what can I do? My brother will be here tomorrow to collect her.

And James is away again. Oh, how I wish he were here.

I replied to Mama's request advising that Charity will be sent tomorrow, but I must have her back next week. I told Charity that she must go. She is still sulking and doesn't want to leave. I must close this book and make plans. Mama wouldn't request my servant unless she was desperate.

James came home two evenings ago and was upset to find Charity gone. I told him I have managed nicely and he need not worry about me for she will be back soon. He was still quite concerned.

"I have been singing to myself so I am quite content!"

And then I began a song Charity usually sings, and poor James feigned a smile. I kept right on singing, as if I did not notice my voice is much like a dog's that insists on howling at the moon. Bless him, he bit his lip and waited until I finished then clapped.

Last night we sat in his library. As the fire warmed us, James informed me the war is escalating. Many Northerners believe our servants should be free. I would not presume to tell James I believe the Northerners to be right, so I only nodded.

And I have battled many sleepless nights worrying about my husband and this trouble. Although I believe in my heart it is not right to own another like one would possess a horse or tea service, how could I ever go against my husband's beliefs?

James often reminds me I do not need to concern myself about matters like these. Yet, I still worry and wonder. Would I free Charity if there were ever a chance?

I do not know!

CHAPTER 9

Magnolia Hall
Greensville, NC
June 2000

Tildy and I are standing in the upstairs hallway. It's hot and muggy, and I'm dripping with sweat. A moment ago Tildy opened the closet door, stood on the small stepladder, pulled a heavy crystal bowl off the shelf and then handed it to me.

"It's hot up here," I say as we walk into the hallway.

Tildy's face is as sweaty as mine. A light breeze kites from the open window at the end of the hall and finds us. I lift my arms in an effort to pull my T-shirt away from my wet skin.

Tildy reaches out and touches the crystal bowl. "This was Miss Charlotte's compote. Her mother gave it to her."

The glass feels cool and smooth against my palms. "Which Charlotte—my father's sister?"

"No, your great-great-grandmama Charlotte, the one whose husband built this house. Oh, how I wish we had her diary. Mr. Grey was positive this was the bowl she wrote about. Seems Charlotte's mama came out from town, brought it to her all wrapped up." Tildy dips her chin a little. "God forgive me, I hid the compote, too."

I think about my uncle and Tildy alone in this house—her rushing around, hiding things, and Grey probably oblivious to all of it.

"Sent me off one day to sell it. I put some money in his checking account so he wouldn't know. I snuck it back in the house in my shopping bag. I couldn't let him get rid of it. I knew deep down inside someone like you would come along."

Her expression is so serious I almost believe her. "Did you really think someone would *come along?*"

She nods. "I did."

"How did you know?"

"God always provides, honey. I wanted to save it because it belongs here. Your relatives loved the bowl. Now you can, too!"

"Tildy, that's ridiculous. It's just a glass bowl, nothing more. And you had no idea about me."

"We all got our beliefs. And memories, too. Don't you have anything you just can't give up?"

I think about the one drawer in my dresser where I kept

a few pictures and some cards. All gone because Bill forgot to empty the drawer. Or maybe he just didn't care.

"What's the matter, honey? You got that worried look on your face again."

"I was just thinking about how my ex took my pictures, little things I was saving."

"Oh, I'm so sorry."

Tildy's voice is clear. I look at her and smile. "Why don't you take the bowl home?" I try to hand the compote to her, but she throws her hands in the air.

"No way. That compote isn't leaving the house. My Lord, this bowl has been here since the beginning. Go stand in the sunshine for a minute."

"What?"

She motions toward the window at the end of the hall. "Go stand in the sunshine with the bowl. I want to make you happy."

Hoping she'll take the thing, I walk down the stretch of hall, find the square of light. "Here?"

"There you go. Now hold that precious bowl out," Tildy calls.

My arms stretch out and the sun seizes the crystal. Inch-long rainbows dance around me and up the walls.

"Look at the sparkles. Just imagine. We're seeing the same light Miss Charlotte and Miss Charity saw."

My physics and math are weak, but I know it's not the

same light. "Tildy, that was a long time... Who's Miss Charity?"

"My great-great-grandmama. I know she must have seen the light, too." She walks to me, gently takes the bowl from my hands, holds it higher and turns it a little. "Imagine Miss Charlotte looking at the bowl, her belly out to here, waiting for her baby."

"I can't. She doesn't seem real to me." But my heart begins to ache and I can't figure out why.

"Mr. Grey, he should have never gotten rid of all his memories. I don't know what he did with the pictures, the letters. He must have thrown them away. I asked him a hundred times if he hid them someplace and he'd just shake his head."

"Don't worry. Really, I don't care." I think about how my mother destroyed all my father's pictures and my heart hurts a little more.

Tildy's hand touches my forearm. "You care. I can tell, even though you won't admit it. That's why the other day you were looking at the picture of Mr. Grey."

"I miss my pictures. My mother burned all the ones of my father. Put them in a bucket on the kitchen table and lit a match. Poof!" My fingers stretch up like fire.

"Why, that's just crazy."

"Tell me about it."

Without warning Tildy hands me the compote again, and

I'm left with the unexpected weight. As if on cue, light reflects from the bowl and rainbow prisms splash around us. I lift the glass higher, for a moment feel like I'm inside a kaleidoscope.

"You got the same touch Miss Charlotte had."

I think about her and wonder what she thought, how she felt seeing this.

"Mr. Grey told me Miss Charlotte worried about her husband, the war, her servant Charity—my relative."

I lift the bowl a little more. "How can you be sure my uncle told you the truth and wasn't making up stories?" I ask, watching the prisms dance against the walls.

"Why would he do that?"

Goose bumps lift on my skin as cool air floats in. "Maybe he didn't, but you don't have proof."

"You sound like my daughter. She tells me Magnolia Hall is just a place some people had before. That I make too much of it. What people don't understand is, this compote holds Miss Charlotte's and Miss Charity's memories." Tildy reaches out, touches the fluted edge and sighs. "Can you imagine my family looked at these rainbows, too?"

"This is just glass, Tildy. That's all."

"We'd better put the bowl back." Tildy goes to the closet and starts to climb the step stool. I look at her. She's so nice and I really like her.

"Wait," I say.

"What, honey?" She turns, smiles.

"Why put it back in the closet? Please, you take it. I'm giving it to you."

"Like I said before, it's not leaving this house."

"Okay, but why leave it in the closet?"

"What do you mean?"

"Let's leave it out, enjoy it."

"You're right. It needs some air, more sunlight. I could put fruit in it."

"Right."

"You take it downstairs and put it on the dining room table." Tildy hands me the crystal bowl. "Be careful now, don't let it slip."

I walk downstairs, place the bowl in the middle of table, realize it does look nice, then go back. "It looks really good on the table."

"That's where it belongs."

My mother never liked crystal—fancy things. And now I wonder if they reminded her of my father's life here.

"Come on, Miss Juliette, we got derailed. I still want to show you something that's more special than anything."

"Tildy—"

"Surprises. You're not going to believe what's up in the attic."

"Probably not."

"You'll find what you need, Miss Juliette. Everybody does. Yes, yes, yes. I've got the hope. You gonna get the wishes."

Magnolia Hall
September 1861

Charity is home!

She stayed three extra days at Mama's to make sure she hadn't caught the influenza, and on the third day I realized it was the first time she and I had ever been apart. Even when I went to Charleston with Mama one fall, Charity came with us to carry bags, take care of my things.

I was so happy to see her. She smiled when she saw me standing on the veranda. Yet when she entered Magnolia Hall, her deposition changed. Now I believe Charity to be ill. She is out of sorts, doesn't smile or sing. And when I sing, she endures and does not utter a word or try to teach me how to carry a tune.

I told James how concerned I am.

"Charlotte, the darky's moods are not your problem."

Even so I wonder if all the talk of war agitated her? I am sure my parents discussed the problem. Or maybe she is wishing for her freedom.

James is consumed with what is happening between the South and North. And I am eaten up with his worry. He paces the halls, fretting, and although he doesn't say, I know he will join the fighting. I do not understand how he could leave our home so easily for the purpose of killing a man. It is very difficult to understand many things about this world because I am a woman. Yet, I wonder how one can fight another on land they share?

If James or Father knew what I have been thinking, they would disown me. And Mama—she has told me many times I must not have any beliefs of my own for James will school me in what is right and wrong. I must have ardent faith in my husband and North Carolina.

Last night James told me to send Charity back to Mama's in exchange for one of her healthy servants. I went into such a state of despair, I do believe I scared my husband, brave as he is. He tried to reason with me by telling me I must not behave like a child.

I should not have acted in such a way. I am not a good wife. Keeping Charity with me, if she is ill, would be wrong and selfish.

Magnolia Hall
Greensville, NC
June 2000

"This door swells sometimes. You'll have to get it fixed soon," Tildy says.

I'm inside the closet again, sweating, trying to open the

door to the attic, and wondering what the hell I'm doing here.

"I don't have time to fix this, too," I say, then pull hard on the door handle. "The new owner can take care of these small repairs. Thank God, the inspector didn't find the attic."

"Magnolia Hall is temperamental. She needs you to show her you want to see the attic. Anybody can visit the first two floors, only *owners* get to go above that."

I stop and look at her. "That's just ridiculous. I know you don't believe that!"

"I do. The inspector didn't see it." Her serious expression stays fixed for a breath and then she smiles. "I'm just telling you stories. Trying to entertain you, honey, since it's so warm."

"I know." I thump the wood panel with my palm. "Open, damn it."

"Work hard and that old door will open."

I pull, tell myself no feelings are in this door, the walls, the house.

"Okay, you tried hard enough." Tildy palms my shoulders, guides me out of the closet and steps in.

I'm soaking wet. The breeze from the open window at the end of the hall finds me. "It's stuck and there's no way—"

Tildy turns the handle, the door opens and musty air wafts out.

"Come on. We've wasted enough time." Tildy starts up the stairs.

"How did you—"

"That door's always been a problem. Don't take it personally. You'll get the hang of it," Tildy calls over her shoulder.

I follow her. "But how did the door open? It was stuck."

"Don't go getting weird on me."

I laugh. "Me, weird? You were the one who—"

"I was kidding. Don't be upset. You just got to know how to pull it the right way. I'll show you later."

We reach the top of the stairs, stop, look around. The attic is empty, a huge space. Sunlight cascades in from two dormers facing east.

"Mr. Grey stopped coming up here when he thought everything was gone." Tildy walks to the other side of the room. "Here's what I want you to see." A white sheet covers a large lump.

"I've never been in an attic." I walk to where she is.

"About time."

A few days ago I was standing in a casino, a building so new I could almost smell the fresh paint.

Tildy lifts the sheet. The white cotton, dustless, floats up then flutters sideways a little before it falls and rests like a dying ghost.

"Isn't it wonderful?" she asks.

A stately wooden cradle, the color of maple syrup, rocks back and forth.

"It is. Where did it come from?"

"Been here forever. Miss Charlotte's husband made it. Mr. Grey forgot about the cradle. Long time ago he told me Miss Charlotte wrote about it in her diary. How she loved it, wanted all the Magnolia Hall babies to be in it. Never wanted it to leave the house."

"Did *you* actually read this diary or did Grey just tell you about it?"

"I didn't read it. Mr. Grey did, though."

"Oh." I wonder if Grey made up stories to placate Tildy, to keep her here.

"He packed up the diary and got rid of all family pictures long before I became the housekeeper. My mama was here then. She told me one day he just gathered it all up, pictures of his sister, your daddy, anything that was family, and the next day they were gone."

"Did your mother ask him why?"

"Back then people didn't ask things like that. She suspected Mr. Grey might put the pictures back out on the mantel after a while."

"Did he?"

"No. When I came to work, I asked him a couple of times if he wanted me to find the pictures, Miss Charlotte's diary. He just shook his head."

Tildy kneels beside the cradle. "All the children of this

house slept right in here." Her hand pats the blanket inside then her fingers brush the rocker's edge, trace the length of it. She sighs, the sound echoing through the room.

"I can still feel the heat from Miss Charlotte's touch."

"You are spooking me now!"

She laughs. "Nothing creepy about Magnolia Hall." She glances up. "You're thinking I'm silly. Sometimes I am. An old lady with her memories, her silliness. But I feel my people's memories up here just as strong as I feel them downstairs."

I go to where she's kneeling. "Maybe you need to take a vacation. See other places. See the country."

"No, I like it right here. You know, Miss Juliette, wood holds memories like glass does. But baby memories, they stay around a lot longer."

"I don't believe that."

"Not enough children were born here. Can't you imagine Miss Charlotte leaning over this cradle tending to her baby?"

My throat feels dry as if it's coated with dust. I don't like peeking into places I don't belong—I'm not part of this house, the family. My mother made sure of that. These are other people's memories, even if we share the same twisted DNA.

"Your grandmother let me borrow the cradle for my baby girl. My great-great-granddaddy lay here, too. Mr. Grey always said my children belonged in this cradle as much as the Alexanders did because we'd been at the house just as long. Why, your daddy slept here. Can you imagine, and now you're standing right there."

In the silence I wonder about Grey, telling Tildy all these things. Then I think about my father—how when I was little he used to come home from work, stand over me, smoothing my hair and tell me he loved me.

"At one time Miss Charlotte put the infants together, her and Charity's babies. One head here, the other here. Feet to head." Tildy looks up. "Black and white babies breathed each other's dreams, each other's breath. Miss Charlotte, she wouldn't allow nothing else."

"How do you know that? From the history books I read, I don't think it could have been all that sweet and nice." My mother talked about how cruel the South was, how mean and small and just disgusting the South could be.

Tildy fingers the yellowed lace pillow at one end of the cradle. "I saved the cradle. Mr. Grey, why, he forgot all about this cradle. I wasn't going to let him sell it to some stranger."

My stomach hurts. "Tildy." I wait for her to look at me, but she doesn't. "Tildy, your people were slaves here. If I were you I'd be angry, want to know the truth, not some crap my uncle made up. I'd leave, burn the place to the ground."

"Well, you aren't me. If I were you I'd think more of myself than you do. I'd think about my family and this house, and love it the way you should."

"These people never wanted to know me, didn't care about me."

She looks up, her face absent of any kind of smile. "Sounds like that was your mama's fault."

"But what about my father? He came back here to visit yet never brought me. Hell, when my mother left California and moved to Vegas I never saw him again. That's the *truth*. Not some stupid story about this cradle, not that crystal bowl, not that warped door."

Tildy sits down. "I choose to remember the good things, what I want to remember."

"You're lying to yourself."

"I'm not the one with all the problems."

Her statement brings me up short. "True. My life is a mess, but at least I'm trying to be honest with myself."

Silence and more light from the windows fills the room. I want to tell her that it hurts me when I think of this family, my father, uncle, even my mother and my shithole life. But I don't because I see the hurt in her eyes.

"The cradle is very nice," I say instead.

"Mr. James cut down a tree from this property, smoothed the wood." Her palm slides over the cradle's edge. "Oh, Miss

Charlotte cares about the babies so much. She really loves them. I bet she'd give anything to have another baby in this house."

Her fingers move down the side of the cradle again. "Right here's where you can feel most of her warmth."

"Oh, Tildy," I whisper.

"Since the first baby." Her hand sets the cradle in motion. "Feel this worn-down part. This is where Miss Charlotte touched and all the women in your family after. I touched here, too. Put your fingers here."

To please her I let her guide my hand to the slight indentation in the wood. Images of Grey Alexander's black-and-white photo, the crystal bowl and the rooms downstairs crowd around me.

"You should have been at Magnolia all your life, honey. I can't believe your daddy didn't bring you back to see us." Tildy whispers as if there's a baby in the cradle.

Something very sad inside me works its way to the surface. Automatically, I shake my head, fight back tears. "Tildy. My mother was different. She didn't care about family, babies. Hell, she could barely stand me."

My mother told me she wasn't meant to have a child— that I had ruined her life. We were standing in the stark living room of the house she bought soon after we moved to Vegas. A house made of stucco, a desert house, with a sandy backyard, a swamp cooler that ran constantly in the summer and pushed mildewed air through the vents. Rocks, cactus and barren land—all stood at attention in our front yard.

"If it wasn't for you, I'd really be something," my mother had said that day, one hand rubbing her cheek, the other resting on her hip. "After I left your father I could have had a career, if it hadn't been for you." She looked above my head, as if I wasn't sitting in front of her.

I believed her, wanted to be so small I didn't exist. Wanted her to have the life she needed instead of me.

"Honey, I'm so glad you're here," Tildy says.

More sunlight explodes around us, dancing across the wood, spotlighting us.

"It's a beautiful day," she whispers.

"Thanks for showing me this, really. I know the cradle means a lot to you. You should take it home," I say, and mean it so much.

"Oh, goodness, I don't have any place in my apartment. Besides it belongs here. It's as much of Magnolia Hall as the walls and doors."

I have no idea what I'm going to do with it when I sell the place. "It seems silly to leave it up here. Someone should own it."

Outside clouds shift again, hide the sun, and the room goes gray.

"You don't even dream anymore, do you?"

I lean forward and look in the cradle. "I have dreams."

"Like what?"

"I want to get a good job, maybe buy another house. Get my life back on track."

"I'm afraid we're going to lose the heat in this wood. You need to learn how to nourish yourself. You just forgot how. That's the reason you came to Magnolia Hall."

I wonder how different I would be if I had lived here, if my parents hadn't driven down the driveway and never stopped until they reached the West Coast. What would my life be like if I'd known my father and these people who made him who he was. My throat starts to burn.

"Are you crying?"

"I don't know," I whisper.

I hear my mother's voice. *You're an idiot to dream.*

I feel foolish because I'm crying and can't stop.

"Everybody makes mistakes."

I pull back, realize I'm still squeezing the edge of the cradle.

"People have to trust in what they don't know. Like Miss Charlotte, she never lost hope."

"You do not know that for sure. You believe in things that you can't be sure of," I say.

"It makes me happy. It could help you, too."

It would be so easy to get lost in what Tildy is telling me. "That's the problem. It won't." I push myself off the floor. "I don't have time for this! I need to concentrate on the house repairs so I can go home."

God! I've been kneeling on a worn attic floor, talking about nothing but crap. I stand, brush my palms against my shorts. When I get to the stairs I stop, tell myself not to turn around but I do.

Tildy is still by the cradle, rocking it.

"Thanks."

She looks up, smiles. "You're welcome, child."

I nod then go down the stairs.

CHAPTER 10

Magnolia Hall
Greensville, NC
June 2000

Tildy climbs in her car, starts the engine then leans out the window. "Don't forget there's fruit salad in the refrigerator for dessert."

"I won't, but I'm gonna get fat."

She laughs, waves and heads off down the driveway.

I sit on the top porch step, watch her taillights disappear. The evening air is cooler and the breeze feels good against my moist skin. A lightning bug springs from the too-high grass. I should get off my expanding butt and mow it. But I kind of like it shaggy. There's hardly any grass in Vegas. Today it was probably ninety-five there, dry and windy. But I don't really know because I haven't read the newspaper or listened to the news.

A homesick feeling starts to crawl around in my stomach. Summer evenings in Vegas are beautiful. The sun melts across the sky like strawberry-and-orange sherbet, and the mountains turn the color of thick plums.

I have this love-hate thing going with Vegas in the summer. At night, when the heat floats up into the sky and disappears, I love where I live. Then the next day, midafternoon when it's a hundred and five, I hate the place, wish I would hit the lottery so I could get the hell out. The city does that to a lot of people. Most want to leave, but most never do. I'm the same—stuck in hell and heaven.

Ron's black BMW crunches the gravel driveway. God, I'd forgotten about him coming over. I shouldn't have called him. He looks toward the porch, sees me. I stand when he climbs out of the car.

"Hi," he says, then smiles. He looks so cool, so together. "How are you?"

"I'm better, really. Thanks for coming out. Sorry I called you this morning. I just flipped out."

He nods like he understands, but I don't think he does. How could he? He probably has had his shit together since he was twelve.

"Did you bring the probate papers?" I ask, sure he has.

"Yeah, they're right—" He pats his suit pocket. His expression goes a little grim. "I thought I put them in here." Ron turns his suit coat out a little. The lining is conservative beige.

"Maybe you left them in your car?"

"Yeah, I did." He goes back to the BMW and a moment later he's standing in front of me again, thick folded papers in hand. "You need to sign in two places."

"Do you have a pen?"

He reaches in his pocket, pulls out one of those expensive black pens, unfolds the papers. "You need to sign all three copies." He hands them to me.

"Should I read them first?"

"You can. They only state you're the sole inheritor of your uncle's estate."

Suddenly I feel embarrassed for not inviting him into the house, offering him something cool to drink. He's been nice enough to drive out here, not make me come downtown.

I fold the papers, look at him. "I'm sorry, we should go inside."

"Do you always apologize?"

"What?"

"This morning you said you were sorry, too."

"I was. I shouldn't have called and bothered you."

"Why not? I'm your attorney?"

"I haven't paid you."

"You will."

"I hope to." I look past Ron, into the yard. The failing sunlight is turning the grass, the trees, everything a light gold, and a chill runs up my back.

Ron looks, too. "It's going to be a nice evening."

I start up the stairs and he follows. "The house isn't air-conditioned, but somehow it's cool in the evening."

"They knew how to build these old places."

I have the urge to tell him that I've about had it with this house, but I don't. I've bitched to him enough.

We walk into the main hallway where it's cool.

"This is nice," he says.

"You haven't been inside?" I ask.

"I have, when I came out to start the car. A woman, the housekeeper was here. Gave me the keys, showed me around."

"That would be Tildy."

"She seemed to take a great interest in the house."

"That's an understatement."

"Why's that?"

"The second day I was here, she insisted on helping. She comes every day. Cooks, cleans, tells me all about the previous owners. And she won't let me forget I'm related to them, either. She's determined I'm going to stay here and we're going to live happily-ever-after at Magnolia Hall."

"I take it that's not your plan?"

I shake my head. "I'm a blackjack dealer from Las Vegas.

I don't belong here. Why don't we go into the kitchen? I can fix you some iced tea, then I'll sign the papers and you can go home. I'm sure you have better things to do than listen to me bitch."

His smile surprises me. "You're honest. I like that."

When we reach the kitchen, I flip on the light, walk to the refrigerator and open it. The cold air feels good against my hot skin, and I fan the door a little.

"You want tea?" I say, and turn. Ron is standing by the kitchen table looking at me.

"No, I'm fine."

"Okay. Why don't you sit down?"

I try to soak up more cool, dry air, take a deep breath. In this light I can see what I think is fatigue on Ron's face, around his eyes. He doesn't look as together as I thought. I pull out Tildy's pitcher of iced tea and pour myself a huge glass.

A moment later I smooth my palm over the documents I've just signed. "Thanks for coming out here again, really."

"No problem." He leans back. "So you have no intention of staying here?"

"No. There's no reason."

"Well, you do have a great house."

"It gives me the creeps."

"Why's that?"

"I guess you could tell by my insane phone call this morning, I'm just not good with house repairs, and this place needs work. I've lived in Las Vegas thirty-five years. Everything is new."

"I've only been there once."

"The town is all lights, glass and desert."

"Right."

"All the old houses are downtown, converted into lawyers' offices."

"Those lawyers, they move in and the neighborhood goes to hell."

I laugh. "I just mean I don't know how to take care of an old house. I don't collect antiques, and with Tildy going on about family, how this house has so much love in it, well, I really need to get back to Vegas."

"If there's a problem with her, you could call the authorities."

The concern in his voice makes me smile.

"No, she's really nice. She just keeps telling me these stories about relatives I don't give a damn about. I don't even know if the stories are true." I stop, and feel shitty for talking about Tildy.

Ron laughs, rubs his forehead. "Southerners like their family history. And they think everyone else should have the same interests."

"Tildy talks about her family, too."

"She's been here a long time?"

"Aeons. I think her great-grandmother was a slave here, and that creeps me out. I just want to go home."

"So go."

"I need to find someone to fix the wall first. I know I sound like I'm bitching again, but a little while ago when I was sitting on the porch I realized I'm homesick."

"That's a pretty normal reaction."

"Would you miss Greensville if you had to leave?"

"Not if it was just for a couple of weeks, to sell a house, find out about my family."

He's right. I'm being a baby.

"You have family here?" I ask, in an attempt to change the subject.

"Sure, I was born and raised here, went to school at Chapel Hill. Came back, joined the practice, found out it's really a small town."

"Doesn't that bother you?"

"You get to know your neighbors, people downtown."

"I have too many skeletons in my closets for a small town."

He smiles. "I'm not trying to convince you."

"I didn't mean to sound defensive. Tildy has been telling me I have to stay, carry on the family name, keep this house and the *love* that's in it."

"What skeletons?"

"What?"

"You said you have skeletons in your closet."

"I've been married three times, which is nothing for Vegas, but I'm sure it would be a big deal here."

"We have our divorces."

"You've been divorced?" pops out before I can stop it. I don't care if he's married, divorced or in-between.

"Yeah, I'm divorced."

"Sorry, it's none of my business."

"I don't mind. Eight years."

"That's a long time."

"And you. How long?"

"Months. It took me a while to scrape the divorce money together."

"Your ex didn't pay some?"

"He didn't pay any. No one could find him, which is probably good, because if I could have found him I'd have been up on murder charges. It's the proverbial he left town with everything he owned and most of what I owned—money, furniture, underwear—kind of story."

"Underwear?"

"He forgot to unpack my drawers. No pun intended. He didn't empty my side of the dresser before he hauled the bedroom furniture away."

"Happens sometimes."

I think about Bill and for the first time I feel sorry for him for being such a liar, so sneaky, such a weak bastard. But I knew who he was long before he left.

"Well, thanks for bringing the papers out," I say, handing them back to him. "Do I get a copy?" I stand to let him know it's okay to leave.

"Yes." He hands me back a set. "What about the wall you need fixed?"

"It's upstairs. I shouldn't have said anything. It's my problem. I'll find some way to fix it. In fact Tildy thinks I should fix it myself."

"I don't mind looking at it." Ron walks out of the kitchen. I follow. When he gets to the stairs, he stops. "So?"

"Okay."

A moment later we stand in the middle of the bedroom staring at the wall. Ron sniffs. "I don't smell mildew."

"Oh, it's there." I walk over to the corner where the inspector pointed. "Right there. See, there's a faint green line that represents my luck," I laugh. "I guess it could be worse."

Ron comes by me, leans forward, runs his hand along the seam.

"I can come over this weekend and fix the wall," he says out of the blue.

"Like you don't have anything better to do." I walk to the middle of the room.

"Why don't you want me to help you?" he asks as we walk into the hall.

"What?"

"Why don't you want me to help you?"

"You're busy, you shouldn't have to." Before we reach the stairs I stop, turn around. "And because I just spent two years with a man who told me so many lies I really don't know what the truth is. I let him handle all the bills, the money, make all the decisions because I'm a dipshit. Then of course he goes and rips me off. I need to learn to do these things myself."

"We still talking about the wall?"

My face feels hot. Shit!

"I'm sorry."

"What for?"

"Because I just told you my sad story in under a minute when all you did was offer to help me. I'm an idiot, okay?" Ron has got to think I'm pretty much crazy by now.

"I can understand how you don't want to depend on someone you hardly know, but I really don't mind helping."

I realize how silly I'm being. Why not accept his help and get out of here? "I know. If you help me I insist on paying you when I sell."

"Okay. If you want. I can do it this weekend."

By the time we get to the front door I'm more relaxed. A moment later he's gone and I look out the window for way too long.

Magnolia Hall
October 1861

Oh, my good Lord! Magnolia Hall is filled with trouble. Charity finally confessed what is wrong with her. We were sewing on the veranda, and suddenly she burst into tears, cried so hard I though she might choke. Now I know why she has been acting like a hurt animal. I am beside myself with rage and anger, and it is all mixed together like a boiling stew.

Charity is with child!

I know these things happen, yet I am worried James will not let Charity stay with me. Charity told me the father is a field hand, but every time I ask her who, she lowers her eyes and mumbles a name I do not understand. Deep in my heart I know she is hiding something.

Oh, my good Lord, James would surely try to rid Charity of the baby and if he does not, he'll send her to the fields.

What am I to do? I must keep myself calm and think. I asked Charity if she has told any of the other servants.

Through her tears she said that I am the only person she has confided in.

Most times when a house servant is with child, she is sent out to the fields before the baby is born. I can't stop thinking. Charity seems so broken. I must not think too much, but I wonder when she became friendly with another servant. She is with me most days and nights.

Charity whispered over and over that she hates the baby. At first I did, too, because of all the turmoil it will cause. I asked her what she did to entice the field hand. She looked at me as if I were the devil and cried more. For the first time since we've been at Magnolia Hall, I grabbed her shoulders and shook her hard, told her she had to take her medicine, be a mother. She fell into a heap on the floor and I thought she had died.

Suddenly I realized what I had done and my heart broke into a thousand pieces for her. And for the unborn child—I truly believe a darky's baby has a soul just like any other child, although some would argue with me.

And tonight I have come to the conclusion that I will make James Alexander understand that no matter what, Charity has to stay with me.

Then we can be happy and continue the way we are. I have rehearsed my story. That Charity has become fond of one of the field workers—that they have an affection for each other and they have been wed in the darky way, by jumping over a broom. James will be angry that he was not consulted first, so I will tell him straight away that she is with child. Time will soften his anger and I will beg that Charity stay at the house, have her baby here so our child will have a playmate. And I will pray about this diligently.

Many times these past few days, I wonder why I am so joyful about my child and poor Charity faces so much grief. I have to believe for her. I keep repeating to myself: "There will be happiness at Magnolia Hall."

Last night in a fit of tears, Charity reported she desires to rid herself of the baby. At first I thought this might be the answer to our prayers. Then suddenly my own child fluttered inside me as if to remind me of life, and then I could not listen to her pleas. When she begged me to help her, I put my hands over my ears and sang loudly so I could not hear her vile request.

Suddenly without warning I began to cry. She comforted me and there was no more talk of that!

Early this morning before the sun graced our home, when I could not sleep, I climbed to the attic, woke Charity and touched her hand. I looked into her eyes and told her we will take care of our children together. Charity cried, maybe fear and grief pouring out of her.

"Mr. James will never allow you to take care of me, Miss Charlotte. He will surely send me away. I'm of no use now. I know he will, he will."

I told her not to worry, I would see to everything. And I will convince Mr. James that all must remain the same.

She just shook her head and wished she were dead.

"Mr. James will never allow it. I'm nothing and no one can do anything about me."

And at that moment, I realized men are not as women are. They have a hardness about them that women do not possess. The Lord has made our lives very different. I didn't tell her I was frightened, too. I do not want to argue with James. And if he doesn't see my side, then she will surely be gone.

Charity gazed at me, didn't say a word. I am so big with child I know Charity must see her own image, what she will be like in a few months. The doctor Mother sent out from Greensville says it will not be long for me.

I cannot let Charity leave my side. She has been with me always, and if the Lord sees fit she will be here forever.

CHAPTER 11

Magnolia Hall
Greensville, NC
June 2000

Tildy is humming and dancing around the dining table with a soft white rag.

"Ron says he'll repair the wall and I can pay him later," I say, then sigh.

"Why don't you repair the wall yourself?" Tildy asks.

"Me! I've never done anything like that."

"You never thought you'd own Magnolia Hall, either. And look at you now. Things change, that's all I know for sure. You need to do it yourself."

"Why? And how the heck can I repair an entire wall?"

"You could do it. I know it." She walks around the table. "Might be good for you. Get involved and feel like you're making something of this place. We could go to

Home Depot to get some advice and what you need—then you could see the town your daddy lived in."

I've seen other people do stuff like that. On my breaks at the Golden Nugget, I watched the Home channel and people were always fixing things. Besides, a cocktail waitress at work remodeled her entire house. I take a deep breath, let myself feel a little excited. "Is Home Depot close?" If I do this myself, I won't owe Ron anything.

"Yes. It's right close. And we could go to town, too. Then you wouldn't have to pay Ron. Save the money."

"You don't have to go with me, just tell me how to get there."

"I'd like to go. Anytime." Tildy claps her hands like I've told her we're going to Disneyland.

Thirty minutes later, Tildy and I are by the carport next to the Buick. Thick, hot air surrounds us.

"Is there enough gas?" She nods toward my uncle's car.

"It's got a half tank. The only place I've gone is the convenience store."

"Ninety degrees is too hot to stop for gas."

When we're in the car, I look over at Tildy.

She smiles. "It's been a long time since I had someone drive me around. I used to ride with Mr. Grey when he went somewhere, helped him carry bags in the house, that sort of thing."

"Then I'm glad I can chauffeur you."

"I hate driving," she says. "I never told anyone that. I just don't like it. I get all jittery when I'm driving."

"Really? Doesn't sound like you."

"We all have our secrets." She lifts her eyebrows, smiles

"I don't mind driving. That's one thing I'm not screwed up about."

"Mr. Grey, he loved his car, loved to drive. When he got to the point he didn't feel well, he quit driving and would call Greensville Cab Company. I used to give him what-for about spending money on a taxi when he had a perfectly good automobile and I could have driven for him. But he wouldn't hear of it."

"Why do you think he was like that?" I ask as I back out, turn the car into the circular driveway.

"He was funny that way. Some things he wanted me to do, some things not. Never would say why, why not. He could be very hardheaded. Like you. You must have inherited that from him." Tildy reaches over and flips on the air, moves the lever to high. "No use perspiring when we got air. Mr. Grey always kept this car in tiptop shape. When he couldn't, I made sure my Alexandria drove it, had the fluids checked, that sort of thing. Your daddy drove this car a time or two, before he passed."

"How do we get to Home Depot?" I say, trying to keep

my mind on what I need to. I don't want to talk or think about my father.

"Home Depot is open twenty-four hours a day. Can you believe that? I never thought I'd see the day where Greensville would have a store open every minute of the day and night and goodness—"

"So which way?"

"We can take Friendly Street all the way down to Market or head out to the highway."

For the first time I feel I'm making some headway on the house. "Highway sounds good, nice and fast. Let's go."

"Then I'm glad you're driving. Those cars just go swish, swish, swish around me. People are always in a hurry. They need to slow down."

I follow her directions and, sooner than I expect we're in the center of Greensville, a mixture of run-down buildings and new offices.

"Stop! There's a spot." Tildy jumps forward, scaring me. She points to an empty space next to a large brick building.

I step on the brake, look at the parking space. "I don't parallel park."

"Why not?" A horn blasts behind us.

"Because I can never get the flippin' car in the space. Isn't there a parking lot?"

"Cost four dollars," she says. "Here all we got to do is

plink in a couple of quarters for hours of time, and it's right where we need to be."

The horn sounds again, longer and harder.

Tildy glances back. "People are waiting. Now pull in here while you have the chance." Tildy reaches over and directs the cool air right on me. "Go on, you can do it."

Three tries later and two feet from the sidewalk, we're in.

"Don't worry about me, I'll walk to the curb, honey," Tildy says, flips off the air conditioner.

"Very funny. At least I made it in."

"You did a great job."

When we're both on the sidewalk, I glance around. "Where's the Home Depot?"

"I thought we'd have lunch first."

"Lunch? We just finished breakfast. And I don't have any cash with me." I leave out the part that I don't have much cash anywhere.

"I have money."

"I can't let you pay for my lunch. God, you've done enough already."

"So put your meal on a credit card. It's not every day I get to come to town for lunch."

"My cards are maxed out."

She looks at me, crosses her arms. "I forgot how much your life is a mess. Good thing you're gonna do the wall yourself. I want to eat at Boo's. I don't get to town much. You can pay me back when we get home."

I've seen this look before and I know she's not going to change her mind. I need her to help me at Home Depot. "If you think my life is a mess, you should see my checkbook. But we'll eat, then it's Home Depot, promise?"

She smiles, nods and walks toward the corner.

Magnolia Hall
December 1861

Our child arrived a week ago. I still cannot believe he came out of me. It is very strange to hold a person in my arms and realize that a few days ago, he was squirming inside my belly.

James thinks he is quite adorable even when he is crying so loudly we can't hear anything else. However, James leaves after a moment of fussing, so he doesn't see his red face and his mouth perpetually open like a baby bird's. For days the child has cried and will not stop unless Charity holds him. She cradles him in her arms and sings and rocks him as if he is her own.

Charity must think about the baby inside her. Neither she nor I talk about such things, but she must worry. Weeks ago I told James about Charity's situation.

When I explained how Charity admired one of the field workers, and how now she was going to have his baby, James's expression clouded, then he asked which field hand, and I stammered that I wasn't sure.

James declared he was going to sell Charity because another baby in the house would be too much trouble.

With his words my heart stopped. This threat made me physically ill. I stammered as fear gripped my entire body, then I began retching.

Suddenly James was over by me and I was mortified for him to see me like that. He comforted me until I could sit quietly.

"Please don't give her away," I stammered.

"She can't stay! We do not need a darky child in the house!"

His words cut me like a knife, but what was sharper was his expression. I drew in a breath. James closed his arms.

"With a baby she will be of no use to you. She has to go. And there will be no discussion."

I gasped so hard I choked. James uncrossed his arms, patted my back gently.

"Please don't make her leave."

All I could think about was Charity and her poor little baby in a strange place.

"Charlotte, she will be more trouble than she is worth, and so will the child."

I began crying again, sobbing hard.

"You are acting like a child. You must leave the management of the darkies to me. These are things you don't understand. You will not get attached to the servants and she will be sold."

His words still ring in my ears. I do not love Charity. She is not my family, could never be my friend. And now I have defied my husband for her. God save my soul.

James took my hand, repeated there were things I did not understand. And we have not spoken a word about it since.

All of this is wedged in my heart like thorns. I am so nervous, I am crying again, big gulping sobs. If only Charity would not be with child, our lives would have been fine, the way it was many months ago. Why did she have to love someone? I should not care what happens to her, but I do.

My child was born blue and would not breathe. Charity wiped his mouth, placed her lips on his tiny ones and puffed life into him. I closed my eyes, helpless, praying the baby would live. Suddenly our child cried out, announcing he had arrived at Magnolia Hall. Charity and I cried along with him then thanked the

Lord for his life. So how can I not care for the one who saved my child?

I have not told her what my husband demanded. I didn't want to upset her, I only said too many times,

"Imagine good things for all of us, Charity."

"I cannot imagine anything, Miss Charlotte."

And yesterday James left for Charleston to inquire about the terrible war. I did not want him to leave, am afraid for him. I miss him in the evenings, when the air is so soft and the sky is like velvet.

"Please do not go," I said once, and wanted to say it again until I saw his expression. Right before he left he told me to stay in bed as the doctor instructed.

I sneak out of bed, hold my child in my arms and touch his small hands to my face and to the walls of our bedroom. His fingers wiggle against the paper flowers. Then I put him back into the cradle James surprised me with. Such a lovely gift for a man to give. I do not think I will ever know my husband fully. He is kind and sweet one moment, turbulent the next. James cut down a tree, smoothed and fitted the wood then rubbed it with beeswax to deepen the color for the cradle.

When he carried it into the house, he said the cradle is for all our babies.

All our babies! Oh, dear.

I should not write these thoughts in ink, only keep them in my heart, yet someday when I wear my gray hair like a hat and my children have children, I might forget how I felt at this moment. These pages will be my map, a reminder of our lives, our home.

Magnolia Hall
Greensville, NC
July 2000

Tildy and I walked over to Boo's, a small restaurant three blocks away from where I managed to park. I'm wringing wet. The humidity must be at least ninety percent. Thank God the restaurant is air-conditioned. Now I'm sitting in a red vinyl booth by the door, my thighs sticking to the seat, waiting for Tildy to come back from the bathroom. I press deeper into the cool vinyl and look around.

Ron Tanner is sitting in a booth across the room. He's dressed like he was the day he picked me up from the airport, white shirt, tie loose, no suit coat. He's counting change into one of those tiny black trays.

He looks up, sees me and smiles. I smile back and he slides out of the booth and crosses the room.

"How are you?" His hand is outstretched and I take it. Cool dry skin.

"I'm okay."

"Just okay?"

I smile again. "No, I'm great, really."

We look at each other for a moment then start talking at the same time, laugh.

"Sorry," I say.

"What's new?"

"Actually I'm headed to Home Depot to get some advice on how to fix the wall." For a quick moment I think I see disappointment in his eyes.

"Thought I was going to fix it?"

"I don't want to bother you. My uncle's housekeeper gave me a pep talk. We're going to eat lunch, then go over there and I'm going to see if I can fix it myself."

"It's a big job."

"Yeah, I know. I just need to do this myself."

"Right. If you need help, you can call me."

"I will," I lie. Tildy is right, I don't need to owe any more money to anyone. I look toward the bathroom, wonder what's taking Tildy so long in the ladies' room. My chest feels tight. Finally she comes out. When she gets to the table, she gives Ron the once-over.

I introduce them, and she and Ron shake hands, acknowledge they've met.

"I'll let you ladies enjoy your lunch. I need to get back to the office." He looks at me. "Remember, I don't mind helping."

"Right. Thanks." I nod and he heads toward the door. I watch him walk out of Boo's. When I turn back Tildy is looking at me.

"Has the waitress come yet?" she asks.

I shake my head, glance around for someone who resembles a waitress. A man in a red apron is standing on the other side of the room. He holds up his hand.

"You two talk for a long time?" she asks.

"No. Just a minute or two."

"So he'll help you with the wall if you need it?"

"You heard him."

"Are you okay?" she asks, staring at me.

I laugh. "Of course, I'm fine."

"You don't look fine."

"What in the world are you talking about?"

"You look all red in the face, flustered."

"It's ninety degrees. I'm probably going to die of heatstroke." I think how I must have looked to Ron, then hate myself for even caring. I run my finger across the Formica table, trace a tiny line through the black specks and wish I were home.

"It's hotter in Nevada," she says. "We can't compete with that heat. You should be used to it."

"It's the humidity."

"What can I get you ladies?" The waiter stands next to the booth, pencil poised against one of those small sherbet-green order pads.

"I'll have a cherry *choke*," Tildy says, and then laughs. "I mean a cherry Coke."

"You gonna eat?" He points to laminated menus in the salt-and-pepper holder by the wall.

Tildy takes one, inspects it. "You still have olive-and-cream-cheese sandwiches! Why, I haven't had an olive-and-cream-cheese sandwich in I don't know when. Mr. Grey loved olive and cream cheese."

"Get one," I say, glad to have something other than Ron to talk about.

"You have one, too?"

"I've never had one."

"Sometimes you have to do things you haven't done before." Tildy looks at the waiter. "We'll have two cherry Cokes and two olive-and-cream-cheese sandwiches on rye. Lots of chips, too."

The waiter leaves and I look at Tildy. "A cherry *choke*?"

We both laugh. I keep on until my eyes water. The world seems so strange and weird right now.

"I always say *choke*," Tildy says.

I wipe my eyes.

"I think about not saying *choke* when I'm getting ready

to order, tell myself not to say choke, and then I say it. Ever have a time when you tell yourself not to do something, then you do it anyway?"

"All the time." I think of Bill and how I told myself not to get serious about him, but I did anyway.

"You're gonna eat an olive-and-cream-cheese sandwich and drink a cherry choke, you paralleled parked, you're gonna fix the wall. You're having a great day."

"Yeah."

"So tell me about Ron," Tildy says, and nods toward the door.

"What's to tell? Lawyer, seems like a nice enough guy, but if I think so he's probably a shithead," I say, and laugh.

"He didn't look like one to me."

"Nice guys or shitheads, they come in all shapes and sizes. As they say, looks can be deceiving."

"And you're afraid you're going to make the same old mistakes again."

"Yes. No, I mean no. I'm not interested in anybody, but if I was, shouldn't I be?"

"I guess. I don't know much about men, just Johnny." She leans forward, elbows on the table. "Your daddy used to come in here."

The restaurant was built in the forties, and it was suffering from a bad, cheap remodel job.

"He and Grey came down here for Cokes and sandwiches on Saturdays. Black folks weren't allowed to come in till after the seventies."

I study her brown face, feel bad I've been snapping at her, cussing when I know she doesn't like it. "That's terrible."

"Yep, sure was."

"Ladies." The waiter places full plates and glasses on the table. "Enjoy."

I run my finger around the edge of the cream cheese hanging off the bread, then put it in my mouth. "Good."

"You bet. Just like life."

Tildy takes a bite of her sandwich. "This is a little bit of heaven, honey. You eating in the same place your daddy did is amazing. Who would have ever thought?"

I stare at the plate-glass window that frames sunshine, try to imagine my father here, know he must have looked out the window and seen the same street, the same bright sun, maybe thought about how it wasn't right Tildy couldn't come in here.

"If you want we can go to the cemetery. Course, there's not really anything there," she says, breaking into my thoughts.

I look back to her then picture my father's grave, the headstone of a person I didn't really know, and wonder what I'd feel.

I shake my head. "What's the point? And I need to get to Home Depot."

"Who do you spend the holidays with?" Tildy asks.

"My ex has a sister, who came up from California for Christmas two years ago."

"You see her anymore?"

"No."

"And your ex-husband?"

"What about him?"

"You over him?"

"Double yes. Believe me." I think about the empty apartment, the embarrassment I felt when I came home and everything was gone, wonder how he could have just left, without a word, a note.

"That's good. But now you don't have anyone for the holidays."

"I'll work a lot when I get home," I say, reminding myself I don't have a job. The fact makes my stomach hurt.

"And what about the holidays?"

"What?" I say, my mouth full. I know what Tildy is trying to get at, but I'm not going there.

"I always think about people alone at the holidays."

"I don't really care about Christmas."

"You don't? Why, that's my favorite time of year. The decorations, everyone so happy."

"A lot of people aren't happy. It's a very high suicide time."

Tildy looks at me and shakes her head. "It's Christmas, the time Jesus was born. It's what you make of it. If a person wants to be happy they can be happy."

"Sometimes it's not as easy as that, Tildy. If you ask me, Christmas is a pain in the ass."

"You should see Greensville. It's real pretty with all the lights. And then up in Winston, they decorate the historical area with so many lights you can't believe it." She reaches over and grabs my hand. "Why, maybe you can come here for the holidays."

"I usually don't get any time off. The bosses give the people with families the day off."

"But you don't have a job, and you have Magno-lia—"

"I'll get a job."

"You could still—"

"Tildy…"

"I know, I know. But you never know. Just look at me." She glances around the restaurant then smiles. "Years back I never thought I'd be sitting in Boo's with you, and here we are just as happy as two peas in a pod."

CHAPTER 12

Magnolia Hall
Greensville, NC
July 2000

I pull the cord on the ancient lawn mower again. The damned thing won't start and now I'm all sweaty. Tildy and I came home about an hour ago. We didn't make it to Home Depot. After lunch she said she felt like she was going to faint. That scared me, so I brought her home, made her lie on the couch with her feet up. Maybe she was faking it, but I was afraid to argue. I changed clothes, came downstairs and hauled the mower out of the shed so at least I'd get something accomplished.

I pull the cord again, and the motor sputters to life for about two seconds as if to tease me then it cuts out.

Damn!

A black Camry pulls into the driveway and when the car

stops a woman gets out. She's tall, coffee-colored, and very majestic. Dark hair frames her beautiful face and almond eyes.

She walks towards me. "I'm Alex, Tildy's daughter."

I nod, but she and Tildy don't look alike. "I'm Juliette."

"Last time I used the mower I had trouble."

"Do you think it's broken?" I ask.

"No, just hard to start."

I can't help but stare. Alex is so beautiful. Her smile is incredibly nice, like Tildy's, yet she's leaner, composed and sophisticated.

"The switch needs to be up. Want me to start it for you?" Without waiting for my answer, she bends down, fools with the switch then pulls the cord.

The engine sputters to life as if to please her. "The switch keeps the idle going."

"Thanks," I yell over the noise.

"No problem. If you want I'll mow the lawn. That's why I came out." Her almond-shaped eyes stay lit. "Mama asked me to give you a hand."

"No, thanks," I yell. So Tildy called her and that's why she wanted to come back home. I feel my face flush and a huge bead of sweat inches its way from my temple. I wipe it with the back of my hand. "I don't mind mowing. I love mowing," I yell.

Alex flips the idle switch and the mower stops. The silence is startling.

"You love to mow? Is that what you said?" Her voice is low, and her right, arched eyebrow raises the slightest bit.

"Not really, but your mother has done so much around here, and I can't have you working, too. Your mother said she wasn't feeling well. You might check on her."

She steps back, concern filling her eyes. "What's wrong with Mama?" She motions toward the house.

"She said she felt like she was going to faint. I made her lie down. I checked on her and she was okay."

"I'll go see about her." Alex turns toward the house then back to me, flips the idle switch, pulls the mower cord and the mind-numbing noise rattles through the air. Alex adjusts the idle. We smile at each other. Alex heads toward Magnolia Hall. I grab the mower with both hands, spin it toward the road and almost lose my balance.

Magnolia Hall
December 1861

James has been so entwined with the battles of war he has not said anything about sending Charity away. I feel the Divine Providence has blessed us for a few days or maybe weeks. Yet I pray that all this trouble ends soon.

With the threat of war, the birth of our child and Charity's problems, everything else seems like such trifling matters. Yesterday I had to contend with being mortified because three women from the Greensville Friendship Club came to call. They wore bright smiles as if North Carolina and our husbands had no trouble.

I do not know how Mama tolerates them. Their one visit has made me fairly beside myself. I am glad I live at Magnolia Hall so I do not have to contend with them on Tuesdays when they meet.

Mama had warned me to be on my guard, that a group from the friendship club would come to see the baby, yet of course I did not listen. If I had, I would not now be sitting in my pineapple rocker with a red face. I am certain I will be the talk of Greensville with these silly women who cannot think of anything else.

Yesterday morning I rose with the birds and the baby's squeal. My son has grown fat and happy. James and I laugh at his mannerisms and how much he eats. My husband is so proud the child does not have a tiny baby's whimper but a healthy wail. He sounds like I imagine an eagle would sound. And because he has such an appetite, he has grown too big for all his buntings.

When I awoke I stuffed a biscuit in my mouth and fed

the baby. I didn't change from my nightgown or put my hair into a neat bun. The morning was so warm I decided that Charity and I would work outside. I told her to bring the cradle out to the veranda. She struggled over her huge belly, so I told her to go out to the veranda and rest, then I pulled the cradle myself.

Moments later with the cool morning soothing him in his cradle, baby Grey fell asleep and we started our sewing.

Mama has said time and time again, I should not let Charity or any servant linger so. I should expect them to do all the sewing, cooking and housekeeping. I should act as the lady of the house. But it is too much for Charity, and besides, I enjoy such work.

Charity and I sat beside the cradle taking turns rocking Grey as we cut and sewed the soft cloth. Many times Charity touched the protruding part of her body, sighed, and a dark look grew in her eyes. We used to laugh so, even when working. Not now.

We did not hear the buggy in between the buzz of the grasshoppers and the birds chirping. The women were upon us too soon, and I could not run into Magnolia Hall. I knew I would look more foolish if I scampered away like a child in my nightgown.

The three women, all from the friendship club,

waved and my heart beat so violently against my ribs I thought one might shatter. I stood and strands of hair around my face disobeyed and danced on the gentle breeze. I almost cursed the air I had loved a moment before.

Charity stood next to me, trembling. I wished she would leave, but she stood there, her gaze down, her hands clasped over her largeness, and my heart broke for her.

As the three women climbed the porch steps, their gazes hopped from me to Charity and their expressions grew horrified. I stuttered a welcome, looked down at the baby and was reminded he was naked!

It is fine for a servant to appear as a child, in stained clothes, hair flying, face hot with blood. Many expect it, but the lady of the house should always be prepared for visitors and her child should be dressed!

I felt Charity's sturdy hand against mine behind the folds of our dresses. It was shaking and something inside me sprang out. I straightened, smoothed my dress, lifted my chin.

I asked Charity to take the baby and dress him, praying there was something to dress him in. Then I invited the women to enter Magnolia Hall.

I excused myself and took the stairs steadily. I returned to the ladies, my hair in a fashionable bun, my fresh dress billowing with a crinoline—a simple yet proper presentation for a visiting call.

Later Charity brought the baby in, wrapped tightly in a blanket for lack of clothes. Bless him, Grey cooed for them and acted as handsome as he could, as if he were trying to make up for his indelicate presentation.

The women began discussing the trouble between the Yankees and the South. Oh, how I wish this talk would stop. I admit I am selfish and terrible. All I can think about is how I want everything back the same. I do not want my husband in battle, and I want Charity the way she was.

The ladies must have thought I was entirely inadequate. My thoughts drifted far from them when their discussion of war started. At least three times they had to call me back to their conversation, asking me what I thought of the trouble.

After they left, I told myself I should feel the utmost shame for not paying attention, for not being ready for their visit. Yet, I did not. When I told James about my encounter with Mama's friends, my cheeks blazed bloodred. I intentionally did not mention Charity being on the porch, so he would not think of her. He laughed so loudly it rattled a window in the parlor and caused the baby to jump.

With raw feelings I began to cry. He touched me gently on the shoulder and claimed he would always think highly of me—especially now. I questioned him, asking what I should write in a message to Mama. Should I write a grand apology? James only laughed again and informed me with a smile, Mama would be questioning me soon enough.

Moments later the conversation turned to what was really plaguing us—the trouble anew. James informed me if the difficulty grows any worse, he will fight. With his words I forgot my own social misfortunes, and Charity's problems. I waited for a moment, hoping to the dear Lord my husband would not mention Charity—say he had found someone to take her, or he was going to send her to Charleston for the market.

Glory hallelujah, he did not say a word!

Magnolia Hall
Greensville, NC
July 2000

Tildy's laughter bounces out the back door and aggravates the hell out of me because I'm hot and tired. I thought she was sick! I left the grass half-cut because the lawn mower stopped in the middle of the yard. I yanked on that damn cord at least twenty times before I gave up.

I look at my hands. A blister, right below my index finger, is starting.

Tildy laughs again. And more exhaustion and frustration churns inside me. I open the screen door and shaded air from the kitchen swirls out, cools my skin. Alex is sitting at the table with iced tea in front of her. She sees me, smiles.

"So you finally decided to come in here and cool off?" Tildy, standing at the sink, calls over her shoulder. "Lawn mower run out of gas?"

"I don't know. It just quit on me." I look at Alex again. She looks so cool, pretty. "I'm thirsty. Do you feel better?"

"You should have let Alex mow for you. That's what she came over here for. She's used to mowing that yard." Tildy turns around, smiles at her daughter. "Right, baby?"

"If she wants to mow the yard, Mama, who am I to stop her?"

I take the iced tea pitcher out of the refrigerator, fan some of the cold air toward me and sigh.

"I didn't say she wasn't capable. That lawn mower has always been finicky. Alexandria, you know how to handle it, that's all." Tildy turns around. "Juliette's from Las Vegas.

Kind of stubborn. But she's what this home's been waiting for since Mr. Grey departed."

"Mama, you're going to spook her with all your talk about this house." Alex takes another sip from the crystal glass, her soft pink lip gloss leaving a shiny stain.

"Just cause you're a doctor doesn't mean you can tell your mama what to do."

Alex tips back her head and laughs. It's a mellow, sweet laugh. "I would never think of doing that. But some people do not believe in this house like you do." She turns to me. "My mother is the only person who is not impressed with my medical degree." She lifts her eyebrows.

"I'm proud. You bet I am. But you're still my baby."

I pour iced tea into the other crystal glass, take a big gulp and sigh. "God, this tastes good."

"If you weren't so stubborn, Alex would be the one saying that. Next time you work in the yard, wear a hat."

"There probably won't be a next time."

Tildy turns back around. "You have to finish the lawn. It looks a sight." She turns to her daughter again. "She keeps saying she's going to sell the house and go back to Las Vegas. Tell her she should stay at Magnolia Hall."

"I think I'll stay out of this."

Tildy clucks her tongue, picks a green bean out of a bowl

and pops the ends off. And for a moment I am jealous of their easy, loving relationship.

"Person can do anything they want to do. Alexandria, you proved that." Tildy holds up another green bean like a torch. "However, you will never be smarter than me. I've got life experience."

"You are right about that," Alex says.

"Juliette, sit down, honey. Why, child, you look like you're ready to blow a gasket from the heat."

I take the chair across from Alex, sigh. Tildy throws handfuls of green beans into a white ceramic bowl and brings them to the table.

"Will you girls snap these for me? Juliette, keep Alexandria company for a minute. I've got to go upstairs. Baby, you staying for supper?"

She shakes her head. "I have a meeting at the university."

"You always have a meeting. You have to eat, too." Tildy places a hand on her daughter's shoulder. "I'll send some food back with you."

"That would be much appreciated."

"Come to supper one night this week." Then without an answer, Tildy leaves.

"My mother, I'm sure you've noticed, is not shy." Alex picks up a green bean, pops off the top then the bottom and lobs it in the bowl. Her nails are polished a pretty peach, filed square, well kept like the rest of her.

I follow her example and for a moment feel like some domestic diva. Before I toss the beheaded bean into the bowl I examine my masterpiece.

"My first snapped bean." I throw it toward the bowl, miss by four inches and it lands next to Alex's little finger. She picks it up and adds it to the small pile.

"Really?"

"My mother was not much of a cook. Our green beans came from cans. I don't cook much, either."

"Neither do I. Don't have time."

"Why don't you stay for dinner? It's the least I can do," I hear myself say.

"The least you can do?" Her dark eyes question me.

"Your mother is working here for free."

She holds up a fully dressed green bean between her thumb and index finger. "My mother told me all about her helping you, you wanting to leave. You might as well let her be. She has done what she wants all her life. Besides, resuscitating this house every day is her hobby."

I grab another bean and snap the ends off. "Why?"

"I think it makes her feel like she has family. It's just me and her, nobody else, no sisters, her mother's gone, father, too, and my mother has always been a big one for family."

I never thought of asking about Tildy's family. "She told me how she met your father."

"Yes, she was very much in love with him. I'm sure you've also heard the bull my mother believes about this house. The way she goes on about Mr. Grey." Her voice goes up a little, sounding a bit like her mother's.

Suddenly I feel dizzy. Maybe it's from the vibration of the lawn mower, the heat, or the combination of the two.

"Are you okay?" Alex asks.

"Fine. A little overwhelmed from the heat, I guess."

Alex picks another bean. She snaps two beans in succession, four quick pops. "You're going back to Las Vegas?"

"As soon as I can get the house up to code and on the market. You wouldn't want to buy a house, would you?"

"No, I have medical school bills, and I'm a G.P. We don't make the money people think we make. Besides, I don't have the same fond memories my mother does."

"Well, I can see why your mother—" I stop, realize I don't know what I'm talking about. I don't understand why Tildy feels the way she does.

"Grey Alexander filled my mother's head with too much fiction. That's another reason she won't let this house go."

"She's always talking about some diary my great-great-grandmother wrote. She says she never read it, but Grey told her about it."

"Exactly. He was a nice man, but at times full of bullshit if you ask me. But she loves the memories, and they keep her happy."

I nod.

Alex smiles. "Grey was okay about most things. He paid my mother well. Always encouraged me to go to school." She pulls another bean out, quickly snaps the ends off then looks at me. "What do you do in Las Vegas? I think you're the first person I've ever met who actually lives there."

"I'm a blackjack dealer."

"Interesting." Alex says this like she's just making conversation.

"Not really. It's a factory job. We kill people's dreams of winning millions."

Her expression shifts. "You know my mother's got her heart set on you staying here."

"I told her I'm not, but she won't believe me."

"That's Mama. She's stubborn. She even used to order Grey Alexander around when she got something in her head."

"She did?"

"Yeah. And he let her. I think it was his weak stab at retribution." Sunlight quickly leaves then washes through the windows again. "So you've got a wall with mildew? That's a pain if you're trying to sell."

"I'm going to do the repairs myself." I pull the last bean out of the bowl and snap the head off.

Magnolia Hall
January 1862

James has been in Charleston for a very long time. In his absence at night I haunt the halls of our home, run my fingers over the wallpaper, outline each magnolia petal. I am torn, for I wish he would come home, yet because of Charity, I want him to stay away until her baby is born.

I have many tasks to keep me busy. Tending to Grey and now Charity are almost more than I can do. She has been ill and weak. She has not said, yet I know she is scared. And she still claims she does not want the baby! If only she had someone to love her. She still won't tell me who the father is. And she is much bigger than I was with Grey. There are days when I look at her and fear she will burst. I try to keep her from sorrow, yet she frowns most of the time. I even sang to her one day, hoping she would laugh, but she covered her ears and moaned.

Most of the time when she and I sit in the parlor, Charity holds Grey. I still hope that her love will grow for her own child. But when I speculate to her on this subject, she says she will not love anyone, ever.

Many times, late at night, I question why events happen, and get no answers. James is my voice of reason; however, I cannot write a word to him about any of this. I do not want to worry him or make him think of Charity.

I was so pitifully stupid when I first became acquainted with these problems. I thought all would work out. Why did I not realize James would feel the way he does? Many times his absences have made me wonder what will happen to all of us if he goes into battle. How will we survive and what will become of us? And I miss my husband, our evenings on the veranda, our time in the library by the fire. And I pray for his safety and his homecoming.

Mama and my brother came to call last Tuesday. I made Charity run to the attic and gave her instructions not to come down until Mama was gone. Poor Charity, Mama stayed for a day and half. I snuck biscuits up to her, claimed to Mama she was out in the fields. Mama started insisting that the baby and I must close Magnolia Hall and come to Greensville.

We will not!

I cannot. And I told her so. What in the world would become of Charity? And this house is now such a comfort to me that I cannot describe. I want my baby to know his home, to understand that he has his mama and a place to be loved.

Magnolia Hall
Greensville, NC
July 2000

The bastard!

I've just kicked the tire on the stupid lawn mower, and my toes and half my foot are stinging. For the past five minutes I've been yanking the cord on the lawn mower, and the damned thing still won't start.

How in the world did Alex start it so easily?

I grab the end of my T-shirt and wipe the sweat off my face for the umpteenth time. After I talked to Alex, I came to the yard, determined I'd finish mowing no matter what. Like an idiot, I kick the wheel with my other foot, grab the rope and yank it again. Nothing! I march across the yard to the front porch, climb the steps, open the door and let it slam behind me. When I reach the stairs, I take them two at a time. I hate this house!

By the time I'm cool enough to think, I'm sitting in the claw-foot bathtub in two feet of rusty water, missing my apartment pool in Vegas.

I sink the white washcloth, drizzle it over my shoulders, breathe.

Fifteen minutes later, I climb out of the tub, stand in the middle of the old bathroom and feel absolutely weird. Why in the world did I think I could come to this house and have everything turn out okay? Nothing in my life ever turns out right!

Magnolia Hall
January 1862

My Lord! Our world has shattered. James came home, only staying long enough to tell me he is going to fight for North Carolina. He then claimed he did not know when he would return.

His departure happened so swiftly, I am surprised I still have my sanity.

CHAPTER 13

Magnolia Hall
Greensville, NC
July 2000

My head is aching and my eyes feel like they have a ton of sand under them. I didn't sleep well last night, and to top everything off, the damned lawn mower is still sitting in the middle of the front lawn. The Green Gardener, I'm not!

"You look like ten miles of bad road, honey. I'll get you some coffee," Tildy says as she gives me a sidelong glance then crosses the kitchen toward the coffeepot.

A moment later she places a cup in front of me. "That's some T-shirt."

I glance down at the two words printed in purple: Men Suck!

"It was funny when my friend gave it to me. Besides, men do suck."

"Some folks might take that saying totally the wrong way."

"But no one's going to see it except me and you. It's a good nightshirt, soft, comforting."

"Be fine if it didn't have that saying. You relax with your coffee. I'm gonna finish the lawn."

"You are not going to mow the lawn!" I say, stand and head toward the open kitchen door. "You didn't feel well. I'll worry about you."

"I'm better today. The sooner I get the lawn done, the faster we can go to Home Depot." She looks at me, lifts her brows. "I've mowed the grass before, and I'm not allowing it to stay the way it is. It looks like trailer trash lives here. Even when Mr. Grey was sick, we made sure the lawn was neat." Again her eyebrows go up. "Alexandria could have finished it yesterday if you weren't so hardheaded."

"I don't need both of you working here for free."

"Don't go fretting. I'm all caught up around the house, exercise will do me good."

"If you can just keep the mower running, I'll push it around the yard," I say, knowing I won't be able to stop her from doing it.

"Fine. We'll get started before it gets too hot. Then we'll go to Home Depot. You come out after you finish your coffee."

"I'll change and be right out. Don't start till I get there."

Tildy turns at the kitchen door. "I got a feeling that attorney is gonna come see you. The way he looked at you in Boo's, he'll be here. So you better burn that T-shirt."

"I told him I was going to do the wall myself."

"He looked at you like he wanted to see you again."

A tiny kernel of something I recognize all too well rises up through my chest and grows into a dime-sized lump.

"What's wrong now?" she asks.

"Nothing."

"Something's bothering you?"

"No. I'll go change."

"I'll see you out there." She opens the door. She's dressed in blue-and-yellow madras shorts that come down to just below her knees, and the tail of her blue golf shirt covers the top half of her butt.

I walk down the front hallway, hear a car door slam and then another. The doorbell rings just as Tildy guns the lawn mower in the back. Damn. What if it's Ron?

The thought makes me feel like an idiot. Through the oblong windows on each side of the door, I see shadows shift on the porch. There's more than one person. I peek out and see three women standing facing the door, expressionless.

I open the door, and they smile. Their pastel expensive-looking suits make them look like Easter eggs in a basket. "Hello," the tallest and blondest of the group says.

"Hello."

"We're here to see Juliette Carlton."

"I'm Juliette."

"You are?" the shortest of the three asks as she stares at my T-shirt logo.

I glance down, realize the shirt cuts high on my thighs. When I look up, the women are still staring at me.

"May we come in?"

"I…I have to get dressed."

"You go ahead. We'll wait."

They step forward and I automatically open the door.

"It's just as I remember it, so lovely, a wonderful home," one woman says as they walk into the hallway.

"Yes, Sarah, it is, isn't it?"

"Are you Realtors?"

"Realtors? No, we just stopped by to say hello," the middle woman in the pink suit says. "We're from the First Ladies Of Greensville. We've been nominated to *the committee*."

"What committee?"

The one in the middle holds out her hand. "I'm Sarah Henderson, and we, the First Ladies, heard you're trying to sell Magnolia Hall. You *are* Juliette Carlton, Grey Alexander's niece?"

I nod and shake her hand.

Three pairs of eyes opened a little wider.

"Well, then," the pink-suited one says, "you can call me Miriam. Everyone does. I'm the president."

"President of what?"

"Clair, you explain the situation?" Miriam says. She looks around the hall. "I do believe this is just a perfect place for us. Won't it be wonderful?"

"Sugar, stay on the subject." Sarah gives Clair's pastel sleeve a tug.

"When we heard you'd inherited Magnolia Hall we called an emergency meeting."

"Why?" I wonder what in the hell these women are talking about.

"May we sit down for a moment?" Clair asks.

"There's not much to sit on. And I need to get dressed."

"This will only take a moment."

Before I can say another word, they walk into the living room and I follow.

"What in the world happened to all of Grey's things?" They stand in the middle of the room and look around. "It's so empty, so…bare," Sarah says, then looks directly at my thighs.

"I'll be right back." I run up the stairs and pull on a pair of jeans, tuck in my shirt and race down to the living room.

"Sorry. Now, explain to me why you're here."

"What happened to all the beautiful furnishings? We peeked in the other room and almost everything is gone!"

"My uncle had to sell some things."

"Some? Why, this house was filled with most beautiful antiques."

I think it's Miriam who says this.

"I can't believe all those lovely things are gone."

"You can believe it. They are. He had a hard time."

Sarah looks around the room again. The rattling hum of the lawn mower stops. Christ, I forgot about Tildy!

"I really need to get—"

"As I was saying, the FLG membership, when they found out you were going to sell Magnolia Hall, had an emergency meeting. We do that only on rare occasions. For the last few days we've been working on funding and we've come up with an idea for the purchase." Sarah's drawl seems thicker than before.

A buyer! A way back to Vegas with money in my pocket to fix my life, buy a house, a new couch.

"We, on behalf of the women's club, would like to make you an offer." Sarah temples her fingers as if in prayer.

"An offer," I say slowly, allowing myself to taste both the wonderful words.

"Yes. We're prepared to buy Magnolia Hall."

"There's a small repair problem," I say, soft-pedaling the wall. They nod.

"Doesn't matter. Our organization is willing to fix any

problem. My husband is in the city manager's office," Miriam says.

"Cool," I say. I am thankful, happy, yet my stomach twists in a way I don't really understand.

"Yes, isn't it...*cool*?" Clair says. "However we were planning on buying the furnishings, too. There's nothing in the garage? Maybe the attic?"

"There's no garage, only a carport."

"The entire house...empty."

I think about the cradle in the attic. Tildy should have it, and the crystal compote, the rocker, what's left of the china. "There's a bed upstairs. I think it's pretty old. That's about it."

"I can't believe Grey would sell everything. Why, he was so fond of his family's heirlooms," Sarah says.

"When was the last time you saw him?" I ask.

"Well, it had been some time.... I heard he was quite ill and Tildy was working here."

"That's what I heard, too," Clair says. "Maybe that explains the furniture loss."

"What would that have to do with it? Tildy has been here most of her life."

Eyes widen again. "For pay, of course."

"Not at the end," I say lamely. "She stayed on because my uncle had no one else."

"What about you?"

"I wasn't here. We weren't close."

"This may not be the time to delve into all this," Miriam says. "We need to talk about Magnolia Hall and the sale. Juliette doesn't have to worry herself about anything. She just lost her uncle."

My heart is slamming against my ribs. "I wasn't close to my uncle, barely knew him."

"We need to get back to what's really important," Clair says, part of her accent gone.

"Yes, don't worry," someone else chimes in.

The lawn mower cuts off again.

"Tildy! I need to get her a glass of water."

Clair is beside me. "Dear, she'll be fine. Now about the house."

"But I'm not even paying her—"

"I think Grey had his problems with her. Poor man treated her like part of the family." Clair leans closer.

My mouth drops open.

"Young Charlotte treated her the same until she went to Atlanta. Then Grey changed so. Talk was—"

Miriam slices her hand through the air like a coach. "Now that *is* idle gossip. My mother always said such nice things about Charlotte, your aunt. Everyone thought so highly of her."

"Let's talk about something fun. Magnolia Hall looks wonderful. Even without furniture, she's beautiful," Sarah says.

"Right! This place is a dump," I say, and stare at Sarah.

The squeak of tennis shoes tells me Tildy is walking down the hall. Sure enough, she comes around the corner, sweat streaking her dark face, shirt and shorts.

"Miss Juliette, you need anything?" She wipes the back of her hand across her forehead.

"No. Thanks for mowing. I was just coming out to bring you some water." I move toward her. "Ladies, this is Matilda Butler."

"I know Tildy," Sarah announces.

"Tildy, join us," I demand.

A surprised look drops into Tildy's dark eyes and the corners of her mouth twitch up in a grin. "I really should—"

I seize Tildy's warm, moist arm. "You really should. These ladies want to buy the house."

"Miss Juliette?"

Miriam clears her throat. "Hi, Tildy. Don't you trouble yourself with all these details."

"Magnolia Hall belongs to Miss Juliette and should stay that way. She's the family. If he'd wanted you ladies to have her—"

"Juliette," Sarah says, and smiles. "Everything's going to be just wonderful."

"Let's get back to the sale." Clair fumbles through her beige Coach handbag and pulls out papers. "My husband, he's in real estate and drew up this agreement—"

"I need to think—" I say for some stupid reason. What do I need to think about? I want to sell the house and these women want to buy. What could be more perfect?

"We really don't have a lot of time. We're due at the meeting. Now if you'll just sign this." Clair thrusts the paper with a pen she's found in her purse. I stare at the line she's pointing to, know if I sign I'll be happy, have money and I can finally fix my life.

Then I make the mistake of looking at Tildy. Lines etch her forehead and her eyes are darker than I've ever seen them.

"I've got something to do in the kitchen," she says, and turns. Before I can say anything, her tennis shoes squeak down the hall.

"It's just as well. She'll find another family to work for," Sarah says.

"She doesn't need to work. She has an IRA and her daughter—"

"Oh, her daughter. I've heard about her. Very well educated. Grey probably took care of that, too."

"No, he didn't. They still are paying off Alex's college debt."

"It's great we can make this deal. Just sign, and we'll get you a check this afternoon."

I nod, take the pen.

"Clair can even take you to the airport when she brings the check out. We're willing to pay you one-hundred thousand dollars and we'll handle everything."

A cool hundred grand. The women circle around me, nod.

"We're planning on turning Magnolia Hall into our headquarters."

"I can't sell!" I blurt.

"What?" Miriam asked.

Something deep inside me wells up and I give Sarah back the pen. "I'm not sure—"

"Now, sugar, you *are* sure. Why, you just sign the paper. It's obvious you're not happy here. We'll take care of everything," Sarah says as she moves closer. "Why bother yourself with anything else? Your uncle wouldn't mind."

She fans the paper at me and I feel the breeze, realize I'm sweating.

"Take it, go on."

As much as I want to, I can't. And the worst part is I don't know why.

"If it's about Tildy, we'll talk to her."

"I can't sign the papers right now."

They follow me into the hall, to the door. "But dear, you said—"

"I need some time to think about all this." The women stare at me. I think about my father living here, all the stories Tildy has told me, and I just can't sign the papers.

Magnolia Hall
February 1862

It has been thirty-one days since I have seen my husband. His only letter promised he'd be home soon, yet I do not believe I will see him in the near future.

I have read his letter so many times, folding it and then opening it again. The paper is starting to wear. He states he misses his wife, his son and Magnolia Hall. He knows our boy has grown, and he will not recognize him when he returns—when the South is victorious over the North.

I never believed my life could be like this—getting our news from the messages Father sends or when people stop for cool well water and to rest their weary bones. From their talk, I know the fighting will not end soon.

And every night I pray my dear husband will walk through the front door, hold me in his arms and press his lips to mine. I should not write these things, yet the war has found in me a hunger for strength and truth. I do not care if people know I want to kiss my husband's lips and lie in his arms.

I have looked over these pages many times, realized how silly I was to fear what others would think of me!

What time I wasted. My childishness is now a ghost who haunts me, walks the halls at night and keeps me from sleep and dreams.

Yet James's letter and this house give me hope. Every day my hand caresses the cradle James fashioned with his hands. I think of his hands against the wood, the same place where mine now touches, and this comforts me.

Mama insisted I come to town and stay with her and Father but I refused. I will not leave our home, and what would I do with Charity? Father would surely send her away. With each day she grows larger, weaker, and I worry so, but I cannot desert her now.

CHAPTER 14

Magnolia Hall
Greensville, NC
July 2000

The women left about five minutes ago and I've found Tildy in the library wiping down a dustless shelf.

"Did you have a nice visit?" Tildy asks without looking at me.

"You know the answer to that question."

"I wasn't sure. Way back, before we started giving things away, some of those ladies came to talk to Mr. Grey about buying Magnolia Hall. He was polite but never let them get close to a deal like you just did. Lordy, this time they actually brought out a contract."

"How do you know I didn't sign it?"

"I just know."

"I should have signed the contract. Oh, God." I sit in the

rocker, think about the money, how it would have changed my life.

"You didn't sign it because the house is becoming a part of you."

"Tildy, you honestly don't believe that?" God. I look around, tell myself I need to call the women back.

"I'm not talking any voodoo or spooky stuff or anything, but this house has memories and I think because you're family, you just know this house belongs to you."

"I don't know anything."

"Then why didn't you sell?"

I close my eyes, take a deep breath and ask myself the same thing. "They just seemed so full of shit, just full of crap." I think about how they talked about Tildy, how their insinuations made me feel so terrible. "And I didn't like the way they talked about you."

"Thank you. They always wanted this house, were mad they couldn't have it." She points to my T-shirt. "I wonder what they thought of the present Ms. Alexander. Probably burst their bubble about the family."

"I guess." We both laugh.

"I need to get back to my life, a job."

"Your life is happening right now. The day they were here with Mr. Grey, I was running up and down the hallway till I thought I'd darn near run out of gas. I carried tea and cookies, then the ladies started in on the sherry. Mr. Grey knew what he was doing. He saved his house for family."

She puts the dust rag on the shelf and walks out of the library.

"Tildy?" I find her standing by the front door, curtain drawn back, looking out the side window.

"Thank goodness, they're gone. Mr. Grey, he stuck by his guns but acted the gentleman all the way. When the ladies left at six, all except the one driving were tanked up like sailors, giggling, holding on to each other. I bet they had a lot of fast-talking to do when they got home to their husbands. Mr. Grey smiled like the cat that caught the canary. Blood is thicker—"

"If they just hadn't started talking about you, I could have taken their offer." I rub my forehead. Tildy's hand finds mine.

"Mr. Grey would be proud of you, honey. Everyone who belongs to this house would be. Young Miss Charlotte, Grey's sister, never wanted to join their club, but time was Mr. Grey insisted."

"That was a long time ago." I rub my forehead again. I'm sweaty, worried I've made one of the worst mistakes of my life.

"They were uppity back then, too. It was because of the likes of them that Mr. Grey felt pressed to send his sister away in the first place. Oh, what a mess that was! That boy Charlotte fell for wasn't the right kind in Mr. Grey's eyes." She nods toward the front yard. "When Charlotte got in that accident, he felt so guilty, he took all her pictures and letters, the diary—"

"Tildy—"

"Got so used to never mentioning young Miss Charlotte around here, it came to be my habit, too." She sighs and walks down the hall.

"That was years ago. We need to forget, go on," I yell from where I'm standing.

She stops, turns and stares at me. "Go on where? You sound like Alexandria. Always wanting to move too fast, thinking of what's going to happen, not what already did. Why I spent my entire life in this home. I have to have good thoughts about this place or my life's a waste, too. All we got when you come down to it is memories. Like memories of your daddy. I'm trying to fill you up with those. Show you he was alive. I want you to know he loved you. Would have been with you if he could."

"You don't know that." I walk into the living room and sit on the couch. The summer I was thirteen, I walked ten blocks to the pay phone in front of Safeway, and by the time I got there I'd sweated through my shirt, my shorts. I'd saved quarters to call my father. I'd found what I thought was my father's phone number in my mother's bottom dresser drawer.

My fingers shook as I punched the numbers and then let it ring and ring until a woman answered. She told me Jim Alexander did not live there. I clutched the phone listening to the dial tone, until a woman with two whiny kids tapped me on my bare arm and told me she needed to call her aunt.

"You okay?" Tildy asks. She's standing in the doorway.

I shake my head. "I won't let myself be locked in the past."

"We all are. Mr. Grey didn't let himself think about young Miss Charlotte and that's what got him in trouble. I should have made him remember her. If he'd have done that then he would have been fine."

"You don't believe that, do you? Maybe he didn't want to wallow in sad memories of his sister."

"He was miserable anyways. He needed his family."

"I never heard from him. It was like I was dead. So he couldn't have needed them too badly."

"I should have found the pictures of Miss Charlotte, made a little place for her so he could think about her, forgive himself, see his mistakes and learn from them. You could do that with your daddy."

Frustration crowds my chest. I have put my father so far

out of my mind, it seems I've dreamed him. Yet, with all this talk, he's creeping back in, peeking his head around corners, showing himself where I don't want to see him.

"Well?" Tildy says.

I don't understand this woman, what she believes in. "God, why didn't I just sign those papers, take the money? They actually wanted to give me a check. I'm crazy."

The sun shifts, sunlight pours through the living-room windows and the room dances to life.

"There's a reason for everything. Mr. Grey threw all his memories away. And he paid for it, a grown man like him sobbing, walking these halls. Well, it was a tough thing to see and hear. So I never said a word, got used to not mentioning young Charlotte's name. I was to blame, too."

"What exactly happened to his sister?" I ask, wishing I could turn this house upside down and shake all the secrets out. I'd look at them, throw them away, and get on with my life.

"Mr. Grey was a sight after he lost Charlotte. My mama tried to help him. I knew Miss Charlotte, too. She was beautiful. Loved everyone, full of fun." Tildy's words are thick with held-back tears. "Before she left, I heard them fighting about the boy she was in love with. She cried so hard I was afraid her heart was going to break."

"A person doesn't just send a sister away because she

makes the mistake of falling in love with a bum." So my aunt fell in love with someone who wasn't right for her, too. I laugh and know I inherited the trait.

"What are you laughing about?"

"Thinking how Charlotte and I are alike in choosing deadbeat men."

"If you'd lived here all your life you would have been just like her."

"She's dead, Tildy."

Tildy turns her head and frowns. "Well, just like her, but alive. After he made Charlotte leave, he didn't care a lick. That's why he got those women tanked up, then wouldn't sell them Magnolia Hall. I think he wanted to get back at them for making him so uppity. There was a time everyone was jealous of the Alexanders for having Magnolia Hall with all the silver, china, the beautiful furniture and memories, never having to sell anything. The Alexanders never had to give away even a tiny part of their lives. Until the cancer got Mr. Grey. That's why you gotta save her, honey." Tildy sighs, crosses her arms.

"Let's have some iced tea. It'll make you feel better," I say.

She nods. We go into the kitchen and Tildy sits at the table. The back door is open and a shaded breeze dances through the room. Right at this moment, I know if I could have chosen a mother, it would be Tildy.

"Years back, I used to think about Miss Charlotte all the time, wondering why she went to Atlanta like Mr. Grey wanted. You look so much like her. Blond, pretty," Tildy explains. We are still sitting in the kitchen, our iced teas are gone and Tildy is telling me about my aunt Charlotte.

"Do you have any idea why she left?" I ask, shouldn't care, but do.

"Mr. Grey said she was going to school. But we knew different just by the way she was acting. It was that boy. Mr. Grey wanted to get her away from him."

Tildy rubs the tip of her index finger over her bottom lip. Alex has the same full bottom lip, the same strong, pretty, dark outline around her mouth.

"Last time I saw Miss Charlotte she was going out the front door to a waiting taxi cab. Mr. Grey wouldn't even drive her to the airport or let no one else take her. He could be a stubborn man sometimes. Your daddy was like that in a way. Get their mind made up about something and that was it."

"I guess we're all stubborn."

"He sat right here." Her thick palm rubs the smooth surface of the table. "Miss Charlotte was crying, but Mr. Grey never said a word, never got up. He was different that way. He should have never made her go."

"Why didn't she come back?"

"A year after Miss Charlotte left, Mr. Grey finally asked her to come home. My mama told me she said no. Mr. Grey never spoke a word about it after that, yet I could see in his eyes he knew he made a big mistake about sending her away. I don't think he ever got over it. Then it was too late. Miss Charlotte was crossing a big boulevard in Atlanta and a car hit her."

Tildy swipes at her eyes and sniffs. "She was sweet and good. So she liked a wild boy? Why, your daddy cried like a baby for weeks. We didn't see much of him or your mama after that. Some say Miss Charlotte threw herself out into the rush of cars. But I don't believe it for a minute. She was stronger than that."

I blink, imagine Charlotte's body lifting over the street like a rag doll, her white, powdery arms and legs flapping.

Even with the warmth of summer, my skin has goose bumps. The house is full of stories—strange family things that are a part of me now, even if I don't want them to be— a history I don't understand. The only memories my mother shared were vague, foggy tales, of people who she thought didn't accept her because she wasn't from the South.

"Oh, Miss Charlotte, she loved her family and Magnolia Hall, but she gave it all up for that boy. I heard he didn't even follow her to Atlanta. He took off. Can you imagine?"

I stare at the table, think about false promises and lies, leaving, and I feel my aunt's sadness.

"At night when I think about her, I pray she found her peace," Tildy whispers.

Magnolia Hall
February 1862

We have more problems than we know what to do with. Charity gave birth seven days ago. Her baby is light, like browned sugar toast and has almond-shaped blue eyes and smooth black hair. I showed my astonishment when I saw him, and now Charity will not speak to me. I stare at the child, then I close my eyes, a deep tiredness filling my body, and tell myself not to think, to just work.

While Charity was giving birth, I stayed by her side. Praise the Lord that Grey slept through most of her ordeal. Poor Charity, she suffered so. I held her hand and tried to comfort her as she did with me. She is still bleeding and looks so ill. She has not moved from her bed in the attic, keeps her back to me. And I am doing my best to take care of her, my child and hers.

James is not here and it is for the best. However, I wish he could take the reins of our runaway life. But then he might send Charity and her child away, and that would be a tragedy.

In her painful delusions, Charity cursed the father

yet never mentioned his name. And in the same breath, she told me her baby is filled with evil!

I gaze upon Charity's infant and I see a sweet child. He very rarely cries and when he looks at me with his innocent eyes my heart melts. Charity nurses her son but not with love. Maybe she will learn to love her baby as I learned to love James. At first she did not want to feed him. Shamefully, in my terror, I slapped her face and told her she must. Finally she allowed the baby to suckle at her breast. But she will not look at him and cries much of the time.

In the cool shadows of late afternoon, I told her she must love her son. She cried out that she did not want a son, especially one to work at Magnolia Hall.

I was so shocked I begged her to tell me who the father is, but she won't. I now realize how wrong our life is. People owning people, misery everywhere. And I cry every night until there are no more tears. Mama sent word again that we must move to Greensville and stay with her and Father because war is coming, but I refused again. I must think of my home and husband, my son and now Charity and her child. What if James came home unexpectedly and I was not at Magnolia Hall? What if a stranger came into the house while I was gone? I must stay and keep our home safe, for it is all we have.

Magnolia Hall
Greensville, NC
July 2000

"You didn't sell Magnolia Hall to those women because you're starting to feel something for her."

Tildy and I are standing in the middle of Greensville cemetery. Earlier this morning when I got up, Tildy was already waiting in the kitchen with breakfast. After I finished eating, she said she was taking me to see my daddy's grave, then we'd go to Home Depot.

For once I didn't argue. Those women and their stupid club made such an awful impression, I wanted to make it up to Tildy. Besides, she had her hands on her hips and wasn't smiling, so I knew it was no use to argue. The only thing I did make her promise was that we'd go to Home Depot for sure.

I went upstairs, pulled on shorts, a T-shirt and flip-flops and we drove out here. The cemetery sits on a hill overlooking the town. Several Alexander headstones are right smack in the middle.

"Alexandria isn't going to believe you came out here with me."

"Why's that?" I squint, visor my eyes and look at her.

"She told me you're afraid to find out anything."

"She didn't say that." I look around then ask, "Afraid of what? She doesn't even know me." It's weird to think they were talking about me.

"She told me I shouldn't get my hopes up about you staying or getting involved in family history."

"She's right about that."

"I told her she needs to have more hope. That child has always been so negative."

I laugh. "The woman *is* a doctor. You need a lot of hope for that, to get through medical school."

"True, but there are times when she should be more positive. Although she is my pride and joy, she sometimes doesn't understand what I see. The girl needs more vision."

I look at the graves, my father's headstone. Wonder if he ever thought I'd be standing here. A cool breeze lifts my hair a little, distracts me, and I tell myself to forget about things that cannot be changed.

I turn to Tildy and smile. "I thought your daughter had plenty of vision."

"Honey, I'm not talking about book learning, I'm talking about knowing about life. Trusting in things, knowing everything is going to be okay." Tildy lowers her gaze for a minute then looks up.

"She's successful, Tildy. I wouldn't think you'd worry about her."

"Her heart's in bad shape…like yours."

"She's realistic about life."

Tildy sits on the edge of my father's grave with a huff. I join her and feel the soft grass and moist earth beneath me.

"She's cynical. And she only worries about where she's going to be in ten years."

"Is that so bad?"

"No one can predict the future. She needs her family history to show her how far she's come."

"She seems happy. I'd leave her alone."

"Besides, she needs to find love 'cause I want to see some grandchildren. I have to tell them the stories of where they came from. If she doesn't hurry up, I won't be able to give that to them."

"Tildy, why would you want them to know Magnolia Hall? I still don't understand that."

"Look at what we survived. My family is in the walls, in the earth out back. Everyone needs to know who they came from."

I think about my mother, her hard-edged life, wish I hadn't known her, worry I could be like her. "Sometimes it's not good, knowing the past."

"You thinking about your mother?" Tildy plucks a blade of grass and tickles my hand.

I nod and look at my father's grave.

"You are half Alexander, too. That makes your life different from hers. Alexandria said you look the type that worries too much."

"She did, did she?"

"She said you're one of those white girls that's all screwed up."

"What? My life's been a little rough…." I pluck at the grass, knowing part of what she said is true.

Tildy looks at me for a long time, shakes her head.

"What?"

"You don't know yourself, do you?"

"Who does?"

"Seems to me you've given bits of yourself away till you don't have any left. Alexandria said she could feel your fear. Said she could smell the fear. Honey, you just need to build yourself up a little."

"Smell the fear! Now that's something new to me. I'm forty, married too many times, without a job. Getting an old house ready to sell is new to me."

She points to my father's grave. "You act like you're the only one who ever made mistakes. So you made a few mistakes. Everybody does. That's why I told you about Mr. Grey and his sister, let you know mistakes are okay. He made them, too."

My heart starts pounding. My mother used to tell me I

needed to get some guts. I was so shy when I was a kid it seemed I was afraid of everything. My skin feels warm. My mother wanted better, smarter, on and on she'd talk and I'd feel smaller and smaller.

"You're a fine woman, you know that, don't you? You're an Alexander, honey. They are strong, strong women. You've got it in your blood."

"If I could just get the house fixed I'd feel better. I know that would make a difference."

"You will. We're going to Home Depot right after this."

"Taking down a wall isn't going to be easy."

"Taking it down is easy. It's putting it up that's hard. Just like life."

"Right! Just knock it down!" I laugh, lean back on an elbow.

"I don't think you should be lying on your father's grave."

I sit up a little then lean back. "It doesn't matter, Tildy. They are gone." I pat the earth, then stand. "Are you ready?"

"Sure," Tildy says.

"I'm going to show you I'm not afraid. That Alexandria can't smell fear on me."

We drive back in silence, my heart aching at the truth.

CHAPTER 15

Magnolia Hall's backyard is full of overgrown shrubs, clipped thick grass. The lawn, the back of Magnolia Hall and Tildy's car all look golden in the early-evening light. The idea that Alex told her mother I'm a wimp still stings. When I watch the news, I wonder how women climb Mount Everest, go down the Amazon in tiny boats. How do women do those things? And Alex, how did she think enough of herself to become a doctor?

A month after Bill left, I watched a show where a woman walked across the United States alone, for God's sake. I don't even go to the mall by myself after three in the afternoon because I'm afraid.

After we left the cemetery, we finally went to Home Depot and I talked to a man who told me I could order drywall, tape and nails. He explained how I could put up a new wall, and how to knock down the mildewed one.

I take a deep breath, go around the car to the shed and

open the door. Golden light falls into the space. The inside of the shed smells like a school gym. The other day, when I dragged the lawn mower out, I remembered seeing a light switch nestled in the rough wall. My fingers touch the switch, click it on.

The lawn mower is squatting where Tildy parked it in the corner. Empty crates sit on the other side. Next to them is a nest of tools, a hammer in the middle. At Home Depot Tildy talked about a crowbar that I don't see. Hell, I'm not even sure what one looks like.

I pick up the hammer, wonder how many hands have wrapped around the handle then I tell myself it doesn't matter—that's Tildy's world. In the corner is what looks like a crowbar. I pick it up, turn out the light and close the door.

The kitchen is empty, immaculate from Tildy cleaning. I have no idea where she is. I walk through the house, up to the bedroom. I lay the crowbar on the floor behind me, wrap my fingers around the hammer and take a deep breath. Tildy's right. What's so difficult about knocking down a wall? People do this all the time. All my life I have been afraid, and today I'm going to take a chance.

I hear the squeak of Tildy's tennis shoes. For some insane reason, I think about Charlotte, my dad's sister, walking down that same hall for the last time, crying, on her way to

Atlanta, and my heart literally aches for her. I grip the hammer tighter and wonder what the hell life is all about.

"Wait!"

I look at Tildy, plant my feet again, know that white plaster dust is going to swirl around the room like snow. The wall needs to come down so I can get on with my life, get out of the past, this craziness.

"Wait!" Tildy shouts.

"Why? You told me to knock it down."

"I know, but I've been thinking. Miss Juliette, you need a plan. You just can't go knocking down walls without a plan. How you gonna get the new wall back up?"

The room is stuffy and hot and my forehead is slick with sweat.

"The man at Home Depot told me what to order for the new wall." My heart pounds more.

"Drywall is heavy, hard to put up. You got to let someone help you do that part. I would but I'm too old." She pats me on the shoulder and walks out.

I put the hammer on the bed. Maybe Tildy is crazy.

"Yes, sir," Tildy calls from the stairs. "This is a record day for Magnolia Hall. My, my, if Mr. Grey could only see you now. Ready to take on the world and Magnolia Hall's problems full throttle."

Magnolia Hall
March 1862

I am sitting in my pineapple rocker in the parlor. The house is quiet, dark except the rustling leaves and the silver glow of moonlight pouring through the windows. I have not lit a candle. I only have a few left, and I must save them.

The quiet night comforts me.

Mama sent word that if she can acquire more candles she will share them with me. I said no, she and Father have more people to worry about than I do.

I have not received a letter from James, but I hear men are fighting and dying. Will this tragedy that has pulled our family apart ever end? Men are coming home with arms and legs missing. They resemble ghosts with their anguished looks, their scarecrow bodies. The sight of them makes me cry. I pray for my husband. I also pray my son will never have to fight his brothers as my husband does.

Soon Magnolia Hall will be the only place where James will find peace. How silly I was when James first brought me here. I did not want to live in his house, didn't know how to love him. What a foolish girl. Every night I beseech the Divine Providence that I will lose that memory. Now I sit alone, wishing.

I read my words from months ago, searching for hope, yet my faith is growing thin. The only sunlight in my life is my son who is like the few field flowers growing in front of Magnolia Hall.

Charity and her baby are still here. She is so weak she very rarely ventures from her bed. And she hasn't named her child yet. She only cries. She does not speak and only holds her son when I force her to. And now it seems like such a trivial matter, when people are dying, suffering so.

One day will I think the same of this war? When James is home, sitting with me on Magnolia Hall's veranda, holding my hand, stroking my hair and watching our child play, will the war be a vague memory?

Magnolia Hall
Greensville, NC
July 2000

I'm sitting in the rocking chair, wishing I hadn't made the phone call. I rub my neck. My hair's still damp from my bath, and a breeze from the open window fans against my skin.

A car pulls into the driveway. I get up, walk down the hall to the front door, know who it is.

Ron's already out of his car and walking toward the house.

I step out onto the porch, and he sees me, stops. For a moment I want to tell him to go home, but that would be stupid and rude.

"Hi, Juliette," he says. My name swirls in the air and finds me at the top of the porch steps. I breathe it in.

"Hello." The small word is thick, warm, like the evening air.

I'm glad you called," he says.

"You are? I would think you'd find this was a pain in the…neck."

He's wearing a black golf shirt, khaki shorts, tennis shoes.

"Not at all. Just get out of the shower?" he asks when he reaches me.

"The bathtub. There's no shower." And right here, with another breath, I realize how much I like him, know I was right to keep him at a distance, but as Tildy said, I have no other choice.

The low afternoon sun shifts, covers us in a hilarious pink sunset as the sun settles against the earth like a ripe plum falling from a tree.

"So we're going to fix the wall?" he asks.

"If it's not too much trouble."

"Not at all. We'll get the new wall up in no time. How about this weekend?"

"That's great. I started to knock down the bedroom wall

but Tildy stopped me. Said I needed a plan. So then I called you." For some reason I want him to know this, want him to realize I tried to do some of the work before I called him. More breeze swirls between us, lifts my hair again.

"She's right," he says. "The easiest part of a project like that is knocking down the plasterboard. Putting up drywall takes two people—that's the hard part." His voice is low, filled with North Carolina.

"Getting two people to do anything together is the hard part."

He laughs, his head back a little. The failing sunlight ignites the air around us, and the last, late brilliance breaks through the magnolias' leafy branches and wraps us in color.

Magnolia Hall
March 1862

I received a missive from James today, and my heart is beating with joy. He believes he will be allowed to come home very soon! If so, he will be at Magnolia Hall in a few weeks. I am shivering with anticipation—my husband, my James, home from the war, away from battle, here to protect us.

His letter is so unlike him. He muses about how soon we will have a night together. How he looks forward to the time when we can be alone in our room! At the bottom of his letter he ordered me in a very bold print to—BURN THIS LETTER IMMEDIATELY.

I will not!

If someone finds his dreamings in days or years from now, what does it matter? It would only prove that love resides in my dear husband's heart. I cannot burn his words, the thoughts from his soul.

And when he returns to Magnolia Hall, I pray he won't have to leave again. He will find I have changed. My hands are no longer soft, my hair no longer kept. I am so thin I resemble a reed. Who knows if he will even recognize me when he sees me on the veranda.

Charity has grown weaker by the day and her son grows stronger and bigger. I am fond of him, yet I do not know what I will do with him when James comes home. Weeks ago I thought someone in the fields might take him, but almost all have left Magnolia Hall. And the four of us are barely surviving.

Magnolia Hall
Greensville, NC
July 2000

Ron, Tildy and I have just finished dinner. While I was talking to Ron on the porch, Tildy came out and gave him her once-over look then asked him to stay for dinner. At first he said no, but she put her foot down and he gave in.

At Tildy's request Ron and I sat on the porch and talked while she finished cooking then she called us into the dining room. Each of us had a different china setting, and Tildy ate with a plastic fork. Ron, in between bites, told Tildy it was the best Southern cooking he'd had in years—he loved the brisket and potatoes, Jell-O salad, green beans and candied carrots.

After, he insisted that Tildy let him do the dishes, and to my surprise, she actually gave in and went home. And now he and I are sitting on the dark porch steps with only the hall light shining through the narrow windows by the door.

Part of me wants to stay out here and talk to him, yet the other half, remembering Bill, wants to run inside and lock the door.

I stand, thinking I might go in.

"It's nice out here. Thanks for dinner," he says.

I lean against one of the porch columns. Ron glances out to the yard. Fireflies leap up, dance above the grass then disappear. I watch his chest expand a little as he turns back. He reaches up, starts to touch my calf with his index finger, but changes his mind.

Go inside, I tell myself.

"Is Magnolia Hall the first house you've ever owned?" he asks, and stands, too.

I shake my head. "I've mostly lived in apartments. My ex lost our house. He didn't pay the mortgage for six months. Loan companies tend to frown on that." I lean back more, sigh.

"And now all of a sudden you own this place, free and clear. Weird world, isn't it?"

"Well, not totally free and clear, but yeah, it is a *weird world*." The air is so cool, the sky pretty. "And then there's me not giving two hoots about the place and Tildy crazy about it."

"Why doesn't she buy it? She certainly thinks enough of it."

"She must not have the money. She has college debt from her daughter, who's a doctor."

Even in the thin light I can see his eyes. They narrow a little, look kind. And I know this man standing by me is nice.

"With med school they probably have at least a hundred grand to pay off," he says. "That's a lot of money. I was pretty lucky with law school, my parents saved."

I wonder about Ron's life, who he was married to, why they split up. Maybe she was someone he knew from grade school and loved for a long time, still loves.

"You think you'll get back with your ex?" I ask before I can stop the words, and right after I'm horrified. I laugh, nervous energy zinging through me. "Sorry, I shouldn't have asked that."

"No problem. My ex and I won't get back together. That part of my life is over."

"I'm pretty much finished with relationships, too," I say.

"I didn't mean I was finished with them. Just with the one my ex and I had. I still think I'll find someone."

"I'd better go in. Thanks for stopping by." I shove my hand at him. He squints, smiles a little, then shakes it.

"Thanks for dinner. Is this my cue to go?" he asks.

"I'm pretty tired," I lie.

"I understand." He walks down the steps to his car. I open the front door and walk in and wish I hadn't said what I just did. I hear his car door close and the engine start. After I pull the curtains back, I watch until his taillights disappear.

Magnolia Hall
Greensville, NC
July 2000

"Tildy, you come out here. We brought you some chow-chow."

Soft, drawling voices float on the humid air into the kitchen. I've come downstairs later than usual. It took me forever to fall asleep last night.

"Tildy, where are you, girl?"

I take a sip of the coffee Tildy made two hours ago and

look out through the kitchen window. Two women, with gray hair, dressed in similar pink jogging suits are standing at the bottom of the porch steps.

"Darling Tildy, we came to visit, honey," one says.

I step out onto the back porch.

"Well, I declare! You are the perfect image of Charlotte Alexander!" The woman's voice is full of debutante hopes, laced with more Southern accent than I've ever heard. Both visor their eyes. "Good morning."

"Hello."

They walk up the steps, one after the other. Pearl earrings dot their smiles and a light wave of rich perfume, maybe Jungle Gardenia, fills the air around me.

"I'm sorry. We are just the rudest. This is Sally Lee and I'm Sally Earline."

I shake each offered hand, wonder why Southerners insist on using the same names over and over again.

"We know it's confusing. Just call me Earl." The taller woman on the right says as if she can read my mind.

"We're old friends of Mr. Grey's and Tildy's. My mother went to school with your grandmother, and my daddy and your granddaddy attended Duke together. My daddy studied the law." Earl is almost breathless when she finishes.

"We keep track of our families, for some insane reason," Sally announces. "If it's not too early, may we come in?"

I don't want company. I run my fingers through my hair, realize I haven't even combed it. "I just got up." Thank goodness I changed out of my sleep T-shirt with the Men Suck saying.

"Oh, my Lord, Sally, I told you this poor girl wouldn't be up and ready for visitors already. It's just too early. We'll go home and come back later. We came by to see if there's anything we could do to help. Those foolish women from the FLG spread it all around Tildy was back at Magnolia Hall, so we knew you'd moved in and we thought you might need some help." Earl dips her gray head a little, as if begging off an invitation for a dance.

They are so nice. I open the door a little. "If you'd like to come in for a minute, please." They both nod and walk in. "Would you like coffee?" I ask.

"That would be delightful."

I find two cups. "Black?"

"Darling, don't go to any trouble for us." Sally pulls a jar out of her bag that looks as if it's filled with green diamonds. "Brought Tildy her favorite chowchow. And you some pound cake."

"Tildy loves both," Earl says.

"So you don't belong to the First Ladies of Greensville?" I ask, and wonder what chowchow is.

"My Lord, nooo. Years ago we did…for our families. Our

families have been here forever, but we don't have time for such nonsense anymore. Excluding people because their families weren't here before the war, how ridiculous."

"Civil War?"

"Revolutionary. The Alexanders have been here since before that. You could be in the club," Earl says.

"Oh, I'm sure they'd get a thrill out of that," I say, laugh. "Please." I motion toward the table.

They sit. Earl pulls out a cake wrapped in foil and pats it. "This recipe has been in my family for years. Just let me know if you want it and I'll make you a copy."

"I don't cook much."

"Then it's lucky you have Tildy. Where is the old girl?" Earl asks.

"I think she's upstairs. She said it's her day to clean the hallway and the bedrooms. Not that there's much left to clean."

Sally and Earl shake their heads at the same time. "Tildy and her cleaning schedule. I don't think she's missed a day in twenty-five years. Except for the weeks she was waiting for you to come home."

"Can you believe the police put her out after all she did for this family? She loves this house like her own child," Sally says.

"Well, maybe not as much as she loves Alexandria. She couldn't love anything or anybody more than her," Earl says. "And Alexandria dislikes this place. I think she'd like nothing better than her mama out of here."

Sally unwraps and slices the pound cake with the knife she's found. "Have you met Tildy's daughter, honey? She has the finest diction I've ever heard. Just perfect."

"Finest what?"

"Diction, you know, pronunciation?" Sally places three pieces of cake on plates. "Alexandria pronounces her words perfectly. My mama always admired that in a woman."

"My, it looks just delicious, Sally," Earl says, and moistens her lips.

"Yes, wonderful." I look at the cake and smile.

"Charlotte loved this recipe."

"I gave it to her right before she left Greensville. Of course I didn't know she wouldn't be coming back, or I would have given her something far more practical. Maybe a travel case or stationery."

Sally places her fork on her plate and peers at me. "*Juliette* is such a fine name, so romantic and all."

"I've never thought of myself as a Juliette," I say.

"Charlotte used to say she wasn't a Charlotte. Your aunt would have loved your name. We spent a lot of time here in those days. Being the youngest, she used to tag along when we'd go out for drives on summer nights just like last night. We'd ride around town with the top down—Earl had an Oldsmobile convertible her daddy bought her for high-school graduation. It was metallic blue, wasn't it, Earl?"

"Not really metallic, although it did have a line of pretty iridescent around the hood. My goodness, my mother would have never allowed metallic. It was more of a robin-egg's blue. Very elegant for a high-school girl. I loved that automobile, but there came a time when I had to sell it. A nice man who lost an eye during the Vietnam war acquired the car."

Sally looks at her friend, eyes wide, mouth open. "That is just the worst thing to say. Why in the world do you have to tell the eye part?"

"It's his history. Daddy always said a person's history is who he is. My land, my father was the best man."

I think about my father, wonder if these women knew him better than Tildy.

"So you both spent time with Charlotte?" I ask instead.

"We spent our young lives with her. Remember how it would get so hot in July and we'd just drive around forever to keep cool?" Sally asks Earl. She nods, smiles.

I like listening to the their voices. Honestly, it's like listening to music.

Earl takes a deep breath and looks at me. "Why, I remember Charlotte looking just like you, the three of us gliding though Greensville, right down Main Street, laughing, radio far too loud. Then we'd turn up Airport Road and watch

planes come in, if there were any. We'd sit on the car hood
when it cooled off and make up stories about all the folks
going places," Earl says.

"We talked about meeting the men of our dreams."

"Like that ever happens. More like nightmares," I let slip
out. They both look at me and blink.

"Charlotte was the one who did most of the talking and
dreaming. From the time she was a little girl, she had such
hopes. Isn't it wonderful you came home and are learning
about your family?"

I breathe in, tell myself not to say anything—I'm tired of
talking about family, this house.

"Mr. Grey always insisted Charlotte come home early—
ten, no later. He was much too strict with her. But I guess
he felt responsible. And your daddy, he stayed out of Charlotte's discipline. He was always such a nice man."

"Did you know him well?" I say, unable to stop myself.

"Oh, about as well as we could know boys back then. He
was quiet. Let Grey do all the talking, mostly. He was a
dreamer like Charlotte. You look a little bit like him, more
like her, though."

"People have told me I look like my mother." I remember when they did, I'd run to my room and stare in the mirror. Now I touch my face.

"I'm sure you do, honey. We never got to meet her. They were here such a short time. I heard she was lovely."

I want to tell them what a beautiful crackpot she was, but thank God I have the sense not to. They are smiling, nodding their heads.

"Remember how we'd pull in the driveway," Earl begins again. "Magnolia Hall was the only house around. Charlotte would run through the hall, tell Grey she was home and then we'd sit on the front porch. She loved to talk about that boy she had a crush on."

Sally leans into the table. "We didn't know how serious she was. Magnolia Hall's porch was responsible for plenty of romance on summer nights. Right, Earl?"

I think about last night with Ron, feel stupid.

"Oh, my yes. Magnolia Hall has a way about itself, doesn't it? This house, with all the devotion it's seen, could wring romance out of Hitler," Earl says.

They are talking about the house like Tildy—as if it possesses a heart and soul.

"Charlotte fell in love," Earl says, and both their faces seem to smooth out, wrinkles disappearing, and they are young for one breath.

"You know Grey barely talked about anything after she died. Thank goodness for Tildy. Why, he would have starved if it hadn't been for Matilda Butler."

"Alexandria, as much as she claims she hates this house, pulled her weight with Mr. Grey's care, too. Always coming over, doing work. If the man hadn't been able to see her go to school and do well, I'm sure he would have left God's green earth sooner than he did. In a way, she was his second chance with Charlotte."

They nod. Earl straightens just a little. "You have a fine family."

"I didn't know them."

They look at me, their faces not showing any surprise. They know.

"Don't you worry, sometimes that happened. Specially after the war," Earl says.

"The Revolutionary War?" I ask.

"No, WWII and Korea, even Vietnam. Why, people met and married, made love and moved all over the world. I've heard of so many Southern girls leaving. Just think of that, Earl?"

"I can't imagine. Well, Juliette, you're home now, and that's all that matters."

"I'm not staying. I have to find a job, get back to my life. I'm selling the house."

"Oh!" they say together.

"You ladies wouldn't be interested in buying Magnolia Hall?"

"Oh my, no. Earl and I bought condos right next to each other, over off Greensville Road."

"We live on very fixed incomes. That's why we couldn't help Mr. Grey."

Earl takes another bite of pound cake, puts her fork down. "You look so much like Charlotte, it's uncanny, honey. Have you seen a picture of her?"

"No, Tildy said Grey threw them all away."

"That's right, he did, after she died."

"Why did she leave?" I ask. I wish I didn't care, but it's like driving past a car wreck.

"She went to school." Earl shakes her head. "I wished she'd stayed here. I don't think she wanted to go."

"Remember, Sally, the time we drove up to Pilot Mountain. A bunch of us planned a picnic. We were laughing and talking, having the best time. There was a Lover's Leap and we all stood by the sign and took a picture. Then Charlotte just burst into tears but wouldn't say why. Not long after, she left for Atlanta."

"Tildy told me there was gossip about—"

"There's always some awful gossip when you get the wrong kind of Southerners in the same room. She said school was the reason, and I believe her. She was a fine young woman. Very brave. She just had the misfortune to love a man her brother didn't approve of—who left her in the end. She told me many times she wanted to make her home right here. She loved this place."

"Not all good things happened here," I say over the lump in my throat.

"What do you mean?"

"Tildy's family were slaves."

Earl stops, takes a deep breath, looks at me and shakes her head. "I try not to think of those things. I remember all the women, garden club, friendship club. FLG had silly hopes for Charlotte, but she had her own dreams. Saved pictures. She was crazy that way. Said she was going to rock her babies in that old, worn-out rocker. She wanted her children to cherish Magnolia Hall. Crazy about your daddy, too. They were close as two peas."

One night, in Vegas when it was so hot and dry no one could breathe, I'd gotten thirsty, gone out to the small kitchen, and found my mother sitting in a metal chair, matches in hand, a bucket on the Formica table, wispy smoke licking the metal, and the flames lighting her face.

When I asked her what she was doing, she said, *"Burning memories."*

That night I saw a dullness in her eyes, hate around her mouth and I knew she was killing my father and his family one more time.

"Do you remember how Charlotte used to press her hands

against the magnolia wallpaper up in her bedroom and say how there's history in the flowers? How her great-great-grandmother had done the same thing? Lord, did she have a laugh, and she'd claim she could feel her ancestors in that wall."

Sally's hand touches her wrinkled chin and her fingers curl.

"Charlotte would dance on her tiptoes while wearing that pink nightdress. Then she'd rest her cheek against the wall. What a sight."

The clock over the stove ticks several times.

"With you here, it's like she's up there right now," Earl whispers. "Charlotte loving this house and you not even wanting it. Funny how things work out."

"She would have loved you," Sally says. She reaches for my hand and holds it for a few moments. Her fingers are cool, her skin like parchment.

Something deep inside me wells up, fills my body. I hear Tildy's tennis shoes squeak against the wood in the hallway, and I turn toward the noise.

"Are you ladies enjoying a little pound cake?" Tildy asks after she enters the kitchen, a smile hanging on her face.

"Tildy," both women cry, rise. They form a circle around her, hugging and laughing.

"My goodness gracious, Earl and I have wanted to see you, but we couldn't come out till now."

They break apart like three pieces of a puzzle and scatter through the kitchen.

"Sit yourselves down and behave. I've got work to do. Don't be fussing over me."

"Have a piece of pound cake." Sally points to her crumb-filled plate.

"Don't tempt me. You know I keep on my schedule. Course, I will have some later."

"Come on, sit with us," I say. Right now Tildy seems like a girl and I want to see more of that.

"Not now."

"I made an extra cake for Alexandria. I know how she loves my family's recipe," Sally says.

I think about Alex. Her strong stare, her eyes, what she said about me.

"Your daughter will love the cake."

"She's a good child," Earl says. "Always was a fine young lady."

I glance from face to face. All three women are staring at me.

"You've met Alexandria?" Sally asks.

"She came out the other day."

Tildy studies me. "What time did Ron leave last night?"

"Right after you did," I lie, don't know why.

"My goodness *gracious*," Earl whispers the last word. "This is just like old times. Like having Charlotte here and the girl talk."

"I have work to do." I stand, try to pull away, but everything I've experienced the past few days wraps around me like vines around a tree.

CHAPTER 16

Magnolia Hall
April 1862

I received a letter from James yesterday. My heart soared when I saw his bold script on the page. It has been so long since I've heard from him, I read his dear words over and over:

Charlotte—I have missed you so.

A friend of Father's, a Mr. Hamilton, brought the letter. Before I reentered the house, I tore it open like a hungry child and ate up all his thoughts as I stood on the veranda.

Then late last night, I sat in the moonstruck parlor and let my fingers trace over the paper and ink. It was as if I could actually feel James's skin on mine, his breath against my lips, as if our hearts were beating as one. Maybe I have gone crazy from worry and work, but I believe I could actually hear his words:

My dear darling wife,

I miss you and think of you and our child night and day. I am so sorry I won't be able to return home, but more trouble is upon us. My regiment has been ordered to move on within six hours. We will probably meet much fighting.

My darling Charlotte, accept this assurance, the only thing I can tell you—the highest happiness I found on earth was my union with you. No matter what you discover about me, what you believe of me, I have always, truly loved you with all the ardor I am capable of.

If anything can bring me back safely to Magnolia Hall, it is you and our son, Grey. And if I cannot come back to you, then know I love you. Touch the walls in rooms where you and I celebrated our love and know we will forever be adjoined.

Charlotte, you are good and kind, and I love you more than you will ever know. When I declared my love I saw you hesitate and I only respected you more for not giving away your heart too easily. And when you began to create a home for us at Magnolia Hall, I found I had made the right decision. Over the months our love grew, and with the birth of our child, sunshine filled our life.

You have only brought happiness into my life, Charlotte—you are brave and strong. Please understand my failings as a man. I never meant to hurt you.

If I do not return to our beloved Magnolia Hall—please know that I loved you.

James Alexander

Magnolia Hall
Greensville, NC
July 2000

My throat is dry and my heart is beating hard. After listening to Earl and Sally talk about my father's sister, I felt dizzy and tired, so I came up to the bedroom. I walked over to the wall, pressed my palms against the faded magnolias and wondered if this was the same place Charlotte had touched, her fingers tracing flowers, before Grey threw her out of this house.

Now the cool paper, layered with late-afternoon shadows, caresses my skin. I close my eyes, imagine a hopeful young woman dancing, twirling through this room, dreaming of love.

I trace the flowers with my fingertips, wonder what she was like. My throat aches, and I press my cheek against the wall, feel so homesick, but for what I don't know.

"Juliette?"

It's Ron. Oh, God.

I turn. He is standing in the doorway. With another man I would be embarrassed, but not with Ron. For some reason I think he'll understand. I step back to the middle of the room.

"I came by to check out the wall, say hello. I knocked, the door was open. What are you doing? Am I interrupting anything?"

"Just me going crazy," I say, and laugh. "No, I was thinking about my aunt and how she used to touch this wall," I explain, nodding toward the flowers, and feel a little stupid. "Tildy's friends told me some stories. Do you believe love can stay in the walls?" I blurt.

"What?"

"I'm being silly. Friends of my uncle told me how he made his sister leave because she loved some boy. It was a bit overwhelming."

"I've got big shoulders if you need to talk."

"I'm not sure what I need." I laugh again. "This house

the repairs, all these people and memories are crowding me out of my own reality." I make myself breathe, try to relax. I do not do well with men, and this situation with Ron has the signs of disaster written all over it.

"I'm being silly. This is silly," I say. "I'm probably just homesick."

"What's silly?"

I don't want to fall into something like I did with Bill, because I'm lonely, afraid. I walk to the window seat.

"The women who knew my aunt told me things about her."

"And?"

"They told me how Grey Alexander made her leave this house because she fell in love with some boy who was wrong for her. It sounds like he was a bum, like my ex-husband." My hands are moist, my heart's beating hard. For some reason, I have to tell someone, and Ron's the only one.

"Everyone makes mistakes."

"I'm silly to even think about it. What does it matter? I'm sure you don't make very many mistakes. Not like I do." My body feels sore with emotion. Ron walks to the middle of the room.

"Sounds like you're having information overload. It's a lot to get a house, new relatives, even if they're dead."

I look at him. "Do you always talk like an attorney?"

"Not always. That wasn't like an attorney. I'm trying to show you my sensitive side. I guess I'm not doing so well."

"You must think I'm an overly emotional woman."

"No." He laughs. "Well, maybe a little. But that's okay."

"You seem so nice."

"I have my moments. But I can be arrogant, bossy. And I am a workaholic."

"I'm in debt up to my eyeballs. My ex left me with all the bills."

"That happens when a person doesn't have a good attorney."

I laugh. "Attila the Hun wouldn't have helped. He tricked me. No, I tricked myself."

"He's a fool."

I shake my head.

"Now you have a house. You can sell it, get a new start."

"I could have sold the house to the women's club, but they acted so snotty about Tildy I just couldn't do that."

"That's why I like you. You stood your ground."

I stand, put my hand on his arm. "I haven't always been like that. But thanks for thinking that. Next month when I'm back in Las Vegas, surviving the heat and looking for a job, I'll remember the nice things you said." I lean closer, like a fool. "But right now Vegas seems very far away."

Without thinking I step closer and press my lips to his. Ron kisses me back and the mystery swirling within me moves faster.

April 1862
Dear Mr. Comtree,

I should have answered your letter of May 27 much sooner. When James Alexander went from here to his new regiment assignment he left but few belongings. I will send to his wife everything I find.

I do not believe the missives from his wife, which you mentioned, were destroyed by him. They must have been put into his trunk which was returned to Greensville.

Of the immediate circumstances attending his death, I know scarcely anything more except on Wednesday night of that week he was here, he gave me a letter for his wife. He was as usual joyful to send a word home.

This was the last time I saw him alive.

What I was told—the men landed at the camp in the early morning light. All were impressed with his constant good judgment and discretion, the perfect command which he had of his soldiers, of his coolness and bravery.

I spent many hours with James Alexander and we talked about his plans, hopes and aspirations for himself and his family. He talked of his wife, son and home on many occasions with true affection.

He possessed a great goodness and I will miss him as I would my own brother.

Yours truly,
C. B. Bradford

CHAPTER 17

Magnolia Hall
Greensville, NC
July 2000

It's nine in the morning and I'm still in bed, mad at myself because I kissed Ron last night. It was just one light kiss, but it was how I felt after that's pissing me off. I thought I'd gotten a grip on this part of my life, but I guess not. This is exactly how the mess with Bill started.

On my second date with Bill I did the same thing. Knew I shouldn't get involved with him but did anyway. I've done this my entire life. Bill and I went out to dinner to a small Italian place between Eastern and Flamingo Road. A lot of locals go there. I knew Bill had been there before because he didn't have to look at the menu. He ordered chicken piccata and a carafe of cabernet for both of us.

I'm not big on Italian, so he leaned over, said I'd probably like the chicken piccata.

"It's sweet, like you."

Oh, brother!

But I did—too much. I washed it down with three glasses of cabernet. That was probably my downfall. I'm a lightweight in the alcohol department. One glass makes me dizzy and wondering what the hell I've been worried about for all these years. And the second glass, well, life seemed just too freaking rosy.

That night my world turned rosy, all right! We ate, Bill talked about his plans for the future, how he was going to work his way up the casino ladder, become a manager. And I let myself believe him. The wine buffed away facts like Bill was thirty-five and had moved around a lot. I knew he was a windbag. Yet, that night I told myself that the man who sat across from me was perfect.

After dinner we drove to my apartment and I asked him in, telling myself I wouldn't kiss him. Yeah, right! I did a lot more than kiss him.

Before I knew what was happening, Bill and I were naked and in bed. I mean, how could I backpedal from there? I didn't want him to think I was a thirtysomething flake or a neurotic tease. So I slept with him—like that was going to make matters better. And of course, since I didn't want to be a slut, I fell in love. Bill snatched on to my out-of-control emotions. And three months later, we went to the Little Chapel of The West and sealed my insanity with a kiss.

And now I'm praying that I don't lose perspective about Ron. He's a friend, no, an acquaintance, that's it. I get out of bed, stand in the middle of the room, and sunlight anoints and dances against my skin.

I stare at the mildewed magnolia wall. All I can think about right now is how at least two women in this house have been hurt by men and one of them is me! I walk over to where I laid the hammer, wrap my fingers around the worn wooden handle and face the magnolias. Did my aunt Charlotte stand in this *very* room, look at these damned flowers with her heart breaking? How she must have hurt when her brother threw her out. How many times has a woman stared at these flat, foolish white shapes, wondering what to do?

I swallow over the lump in my throat, bring the hammer above my head, and with all the concentrated strength I have, I connect with the wall. A small horseshoe mark disfigures one of the faded flowers. Tildy told me if I tore down the wall, it would be a first for Magnolia Hall. I look at the indention—a first for the women in this town.

I swing the hammer again, connect, and the wall cracks. My muscles tense. A puff of dust swirls out through the tiny fissure. I pound at the wall and more plaster shatters. Breathing hard, I attack the next section. My fingers vibrate with every swing and I lick my lips and taste bitter lime dust.

Moments later I put the hammer on the bed, remember I'm naked. I pull on my clothes from last night, then I go back to the torn wall and inspect some of the exposed boards. They are mossy green and smell musty. Guess Clay was right. I pull off the loose pieces of wall and throw them on the floor.

"My goodness, girl, what have you done? I heard the noise and…"

I startle, turn around. Tildy is standing in the doorway, her brown eyes wide, her mouth open.

"I decided to take down the wall," I say, and realize my voice is trembling a bit.

"Oh my. Why now, so fast? What happened?"

I go to the bed, sit on the edge. Tildy comes to the middle of the room. She looks a little shaken.

"I used to sit right where you are, with Miss Charlotte, and we'd count magnolias and talk about things. Now they're disappearing."

I glance at what I've done, feel weird, like I've stepped off a curb, stumbling toward traffic and can't stop myself.

"The hard part's going to be putting up the drywall."

"Thought that attorney was going to help you."

"Who knows if he'll do what he said?" I say, finally admitting to myself I'm fearful Ron might not come back. I shouldn't have kissed him.

"Oh, he'll come back. I saw the way he looks at you. He likes you. I'll make up the solution to wash the wood. After you pull down the rest of the wall, you have to get rid of the mildew," Tildy declares.

"I can make it," I say. "Tildy?"

Her dark eyes find me. "What, honey?"

"Do you think it would be a mistake if I like Ron as a friend?"

A soft laugh fills the room. "You want to talk about that now? No, I think he's a nice man. Kind of reminds me of my Johnny. I think you'll be okay."

"What was Johnny like?" I ask, wondering why she thinks Ron is like Johnny, someone she thought so much of.

"He was in the army when I met him. Handsome like Alexandria is pretty. Nice eyes. His hair was dark, velvety. I knew we'd have beautiful babies."

"But why does he remind you of Ron?"

"He's nice, calm. We met by coincidence. He was buying shoe polish. We got to talking." Tildy's chin drops a little.

I lick my bottom lip, again taste the sour dust from the wall.

"We loved each other. It was simple. Everything I've been telling you about."

"You knew right away? It wasn't just something you pretended was true?"

"Pretended? What are you talking about?"

"How did you know he was the right one, that you weren't lying to yourself?"

"I just knew. You can't lie about a thing like that."

I think about how many times I have, that I knew something wasn't right with Bill, yet I didn't listen. "Did you marry?" I ask.

"Yes. My mama would have never forgiven me if we didn't. We loved each other." Her expression turns to that of a girl, her brown eyes softer than I've ever seen them. "We appreciated love back then, honored it."

"Then what happened?"

"He was sent overseas. Lord, did I love that man. Thought my heart was going to break. Before he went, he came to Magnolia Hall right before I got off work. He waited and when I came out, he looked up at me and shook his head and said, 'My, my, my.' That's all. When he brought me home late that night, he promised me a house just like Magnolia Hall. Said we'd live in high cotton. I let him dream. Deep down I knew he wouldn't be coming home."

She looks at the wall again. "I always felt close to both Charlottes in that way. And we all three looked at those magnolia flowers, thinking about our lost men, but in different ways, different wars. And now you. You can't hide love or a loss." She ducks her head a little and smiles. "I'll go make up that solution. Then I'll dust in here when you're finished."

"No, I'll do it all. I need to."

"If you want to. It might be good for you. Besides, it's my day to clean the parlor and the dining room. My goodness, this dust is going to creep downstairs and cause a terrible mess." She gets off the bed and heads for the door, then looks back. "This might mean you're staying."

"No, I don't think so."

After she is far down the hall, I go to the wall, look inside at the mildew. Against the floorboards is a large paper bag, folded, satchel-like, stapled and covered in plaster dust. I reach down gingerly, and pull it up and out. An open staple, sharp, sinks into my finger and a little red circle grows on the bag.

Magnolia Hall
April 1862

My heart is breaking into a thousand bloody pieces. I grieve for my dead husband, for my son who will not know his father and now for my innocent ways—believing everything anyone told me!

When Charity heard of James's death she wailed and held her child and moaned its father was dead. I now know why she did not tell me the truth, why she was so sad, did not want to live.

I do not understand life. I ache inside for Charity's baby, too. And at night I imagine my husband with Charity, grunting, sweating over her and I want to burn the thoughts out of my head with a hot poker.

It is said women must accept the ways of men, but I do not know how we can do this.

I have taken care of her, leaving the babies sleeping in the cradle. I am so numb and tired I could not cry, have not cried, could barely speak. One moment I imagine slapping Charity, the next soothing her. My heart aches at how she had to hide her secrets from me. How she must have suffered.

I will never reveal what has happened, and I am sure she will not either. With James gone, we will now have to fend for ourselves. And with all our troubles, who will notice an extra hungry mouth or a mulatto child. If anyone bothers to inquire, I will tell him or her he is one of the runaway servants' children. And what does it matter now anyway?

Mama said I am foolish for staying here, yet I do not care. Both children must know Magnolia Hall, for in this way they will realize where they came from. The house is where James spun his dreams. Where I found love and now lost it. The house holds all our memories, good and bad—they are ours. How could I ever give them up?

Even though my husband fell to his desires, I miss him. James's memory will always be here, and when the breeze drifts in through the windows, I will look for peace.

Magnolia Hall
April 1862

> Mrs. James Alexander:
> I have been advised that all your husband's things have been shipped to you. Now let me ask a favor. I should like very much to be permitted to keep a memento of his—a sword which was presented to him in Raleigh. It is a common officer's sword. I will be many times obliged to you if you can give it to me as it will remind me of him and our friendship.
>   C. B. Bradford

Magnolia Hall
Greensville, NC
July 2000

"I found this behind the wall," I say to Tildy when she walks back into the bedroom. I hold up the gritty brown paper bag, sit on the dusty floor and begin pulling out staples.

"What in the world was that doing in there?"

"I have no idea. Probably just trash that fell from the attic."

"I never saw anything like that. And we never allowed any trash in the attic. I know everything that has anything to do with this house, and that doesn't look familiar."

Tildy is standing by the bed, and I look inside, pull out a black-and-white photo. The image stares back, a woman, who looks somewhat like a younger version of me, standing on the porch, dressed in a crisp suit. I draw a dusty finger over her face, let her expression appear again little by little. Her smile says she's expecting the best out of life.

Tildy leans over me. "Oh, my! Why that's Miss Charlotte, your aunt."

I swallow hard, stare. "When do you think this was taken?"

"Lord, that's one of the pictures Mr. Grey took off the parlor table. That was the Easter right before everything turned bad. I thought he threw all the pictures away!" Tildy sits beside me. "Look at Miss Charlotte, in all her beautiful glory."

I shake out the heavy contents of the bag and it rains to the floor. Pictures of Grey with Charlotte, with Tildy, a young woman, a child, a baby. Over and over I enter the past.

"Why, look at these letters," Tildy says. She brushes pictures away and picks up a yellowing envelope.

An entire life sealed in a paper bag behind a magnolia wall. I thumb through a small book, fan the yellowing pages, know instinctively it's the diary Tildy told me about.

"So they were here in the house all along," I say, and breathe out. "Behind that wall. That's where Grey hid them."

"It's no wonder I couldn't find them." Tildy leans back and looks at me. "Why, Miss Juliette, you rescued Miss Charlotte. Now she can come home, stay here forever."

I carefully pick up a handful of pictures.

"Look at all these letters. My lord, Mr. Grey saved them all. And maybe this is the first Miss Charlotte's diary." Tildy grabs the book beside me, and envelopes addressed to Grey Alexander fall off my lap onto the floor. Some of the envelopes are typed and a few are written in a small, feminine hand.

"That's young Charlotte's writing." Tildy points to one. "And that's your daddy's."

I stare at the ink, pick up her envelope.

My aunt made her As just like I do—a flourish at the beginning, dropping down at the end, not attached to any other letter.

"Should we read one?" Tildy asks. Her voice is soft as she takes a letter. "This is addressed to Miss Charlotte. Says here from the Crest Agency. Three-oh-six Cherry Hill Road, Atlanta, Georgia. Guess that's where she lived."

"Should we read it?" I ask, then realize Tildy has said this already.

"Go ahead. She wouldn't mind—you found her, open it. My lord, you are the closest thing to a child for her—you're her niece." Tildy hands me the envelope.

I lift the flap and pull out the page inside, scan the words. Charlotte needed to sign papers right away because the agency had found a home for her unborn baby—a home out west where the new mother had promised to keep the name that Miss Alexander had picked—Juliette.

Familiarity roams my body then clutches my throat. Juliette—my name? I think about my aunt so alone in Atlanta having a baby. I read the words to Tildy, feel as if someone else is speaking.

"She had a baby?" Tildy whispers. "I always wondered, but I put such a thing out of my mind. Mr. Grey never said. I always wanted to remember her as young, happy. And the name…" Tildy looks at me, her eyes wide.

"Wouldn't someone have told me? Someone would have said something to me, don't you think?" I stop, and realize how this house, this family is so full of secrets.

"Here's more solution, Miss Juliette." Tildy walks into the bedroom with a plastic dishpan, the sudsy water sloshing. The sharp scent of Lysol fills the room.

Hours ago Tildy and I read one more letter that was from the adoption agency telling Charlotte that her baby was fine. I began to feel so weird, so angry, I had to stand up and do something. So I got up, told Tildy I didn't want to know any more or read any more, and I marched to the wall, grabbed the hammer and knocked down the remaining plasterboard. Tildy watched me for the longest time, didn't help, neither of us saying a word, which is odd for her. I guess she was trying to do what I was, digest that I might be Charlotte's daughter. That Charlotte and the boy she loved had a baby together, the boy that Grey didn't want her to be with.

When I finished knocking down the wall, I was breathless, aching inside and out. I hadn't noticed Tildy had left the room. I walked through the house calling her, but I couldn't find her. Her car was gone, and my chest hurt more. In a daze, I picked up more chunks of plasterboard and carted it downstairs, swept, then took a bath. Now my calves are aching from going up and down the stairs so many times. Tildy came back a half hour ago, told me she'd been to Miss Charlotte's grave to say a few peaceful words.

"Brought another sponge with me so I wouldn't have to make a second trip. Are you getting enough Lysol on the wood? Do it twice. When it dries, which will take a day or two, the mildew will be gone." I nod and place the dishpan by the wall, won't let myself think about my aunt, how some things now in my life make sense, others still don't.

"When I first saw you I suspected something out of the ordinary because you look so much like her, but I lied to myself. I should have known, I should have sensed something, maybe said something. Oh, why didn't I?" Tildy asks for the third time. "That boy she loved, he's your daddy." She looks hard at me. "You have his eyes. I remember his eyes, and they're like yours."

"It doesn't matter and you've got to stop talking about all this. Please. I can't think about it anymore." I turn, put my hands together in the middle of my chest as if I'm praying, but I know she's right. "We don't know what's true. The entire family is gone except me. So she wanted to name her baby Juliette? Maybe my father mentioned it to my mother, and my mother, the nut that she was, decided to use it."

"It's just too much of a coincidence. I can't believe she was in Atlanta all by herself, and you might have been there, poor little—"

"Tildy, please." I move my prayerful hands up and down. Before she can speak, we both hear a car pull into the driveway.

"Who could that be?" Tildy looks at me.

I shrug. "Maybe it's Alex, or the ladies club back for round two."

"Alexandria was going to Durham today." Tildy goes downstairs and I hear the front door open, then whispers and footsteps coming up.

"Welcome to Demolition Derby," Tildy says as she enters the bedroom.

Ron is standing behind her. "Hello, Juliette."

"I couldn't sleep this morning," I say stupidly.

"I went to Home Depot, checked your order. You've got the right amount of plasterboard, nails and tape ordered for the wall." He walks the length of the room. "I came over to help you knock down the wall. Looks like you beat me to it."

Sunlight dashes in through the windows, turning the room a dazzling white for a moment.

Tildy clears her throat. "I'll go down and finish my work."

When she's gone, Ron nods toward the demolished wall. "Good job."

"Thanks." I dust my hands. "I'm all dirty."

"Tildy mentioned the letter, the name thing. It could be a coincidence."

I shake my head for so many reasons, knowing deep down that my name is probably not a coincidence, and I'm afraid if I talk about all this I'll start crying.

"I don't want to talk about that right now. I can't."

"Okay. You did a good job," he says again, and nods toward the wall.

"You're too nice. After last night, me kissing you, I had to do something."

"Of course. Always the reaction I get after I've kissed a woman. Knock a wall down! Remind me never to make out with you—you might blow up the place."

CHAPTER 18

Magnolia Hall
Greensville, NC
July 2000

It's been two days since I found the bag of pictures, letters and Charlotte's diary. That afternoon, after Ron left, Tildy said that finding the bag proved that a great new day is always just around the corner. But the only thing it proved to me was just how shitty life can turn. I'm angry and confused and feel like the earth came to a screeching halt but I'm still flying through the air. I haven't had the guts to look through the rest of the pictures, read any more letters or even thumb through the old diary.

A little while ago, Ron cut the last piece of drywall, and I helped him nail it up. Then we finished taping the wall. This evening, I'm painting it white. No more flowers. Just clean white paint. Ron and I haven't kissed again, and I'm glad for that, although I've had about twenty million urges to do so. But I'm proud of myself for holding back—I don't need anything else to think or worry about.

"I've got everything in the car," Ron says as he brushes his hands against his shorts. He offered to take some stuff back to Home Depot and I'm letting him. We are standing in the yard, and sunset is drenching everything in a pink haze.

"Thanks again. I couldn't have done it without you," I say, and extend my hand.

Ron looks down at my hand, hesitates then shakes it and laughs. "It wasn't bad at all. Sure you don't need help painting?"

"Nope, thanks anyway."

He looks at the sky and then back to me. "So what's next?"

"I'll call the inspector tomorrow morning, then I'll list with a Realtor. As soon as that's done, I'm leaving. Flying home. I don't care who buys the house. I want to go home and sort my life out."

"I meant what are you doing tonight?"

"Oh. Painting the wall."

"That shouldn't take the entire night."

For some reason—maybe it's his voice or the way he looks at me—a lump is forming in my throat.

"I'll come back tonight and help paint. Or as your attorney, if you want me to go through the letters and try to get some more information I will," he offers.

"Thanks, I'm not sure what I want to do." Ron is so sweet. Last night, over and over, I told myself I shouldn't care who my mother and father were. But deep down I know I'm lying to myself. I do.

"If we get to the truth before you leave, I can find out some things if you need me to."

By *things* I know he means that if Charlotte is my mother, then what is my father's name?

"Maybe you're right. I should read them before I leave, find out for sure, but you know, right now, I don't care."

"If it were me, I'd want to know. Just for legal reasons. Your father might be a millionaire."

"Said like a real attorney. I'm forty—I don't need a father. Besides, I had one."

The drifting sunset has turned everything golden. And suddenly I realize I don't want to be alone, and I don't want to paint the stupid wall.

"Why don't you come in, wash up before you go home?"

Ron turns. "I'd like to go home, shower, come back and take you to dinner because I like you, Juliette. That's okay, isn't it?"

"I'm leaving in a few days."

"You've been going to leave in a few days for two weeks."

I laugh, know I shouldn't say yes to dinner, but I do.

Magnolia Hall
Greensville, NC
July 2000

Ron and I are standing in the library. When he came back, I insisted we stay here and eat the food Tildy had stacked in the refrigerator. I know Ron likes Tildy's cooking and it's the least I could do. He agreed, drove down to the Quick Stop and bought a bottle of Sutter Home Chablis then helped me set the table. After we ate, we cleared the table, found our way into the library, glasses of wine in hand. The paper bag full of letters loomed in the corner. Ron offered again to help me read the letters if I wanted.

I shook my head, then all of a sudden I knew what I had to do. I headed for the kitchen, grabbed the wine bottle, poured another glass and drank half of it, then brought it back to the library.

"*Lesse* do it," I say, faking a stupid Mexican accent, I guess from nerves. "*Lesse* just do it. It's like ripping off a bandage. All at once, endure the pain, then it's over."

"Might not be so painful." Ron picks up a yellowed envelope. "This one is from James Alexander to Grey Alexander," Ron says, and hands it to me.

I look at the envelope; the addresses are in bold print. "From my father to my uncle."

"Want me to read it?"

I nod. "Just not out loud."

He unfolds the letter, scans the page then looks at me.

"Well?" My heart is pounding.

"According to this, you are Charlotte's daughter. James says so in this letter. He didn't want you to be adopted by strangers, and your biological father didn't want the responsibility."

My stomach twists into a tight little knot and I take a deep breath. "Deep down I knew that." I slip the letter from his hand, read the words.

It's best I break all ties with Juliette and her mother. When I look at Juliette, I think of Charlotte and the memories are too painful. I'm her uncle, not her father, and my wife wants this kept a secret.

"Oh" comes out in a little croak.

Ron looks down at the page I'm holding, touches the edge with his index finger. "Men sometimes don't know what they're saying, feeling. They have a tendency to avoid emotional situations. He wrote that letter a long time ago. It had to have been tough. He wanted to tell you the truth."

"Tough? For who? Him? What about me?" I point to his words. "And that's exactly what he did. He never saw me, never changed his mind, never had the decency to tell me.

He just gave me away to my mother—like a puppy being passed around. My mother was such a shit—he knew that—and now I know why she didn't like me."

I start to cry. Not nice little sobs but huge, choking wet grunts from deep inside me. "Why didn't they tell me the truth? Why didn't he see me? I couldn't help I wasn't his daughter."

Ron moves closer, puts both hands on my shoulders. "We probably will never know. This wasn't such a hot idea. Maybe we need to take a break. You could talk to a professional—"

"We just started," I say through a sob, realize I can't stop crying. I feel a terrible rush of crazy energy running through my body, dragging me through all the secrets. I bury my face against Ron's shirt, thoroughly wet the material with tears and snot. My eyes are starting to feel like two puffy slits. "I'd better go upstairs," I manage.

A moment later I splash cold water on my numb face and feel like I've acted like a complete idiot. I sit on the toilet, holding a towel on my face. I'm going to stay right where I am until Ron gets tired of waiting and goes home.

There's a tap on the door.

"Are you okay?"

I push back my hair. "I don't know."

"Want me to leave?"

"It's not locked. You can come in."

Ron opens the door and stands by the doorjamb. "I'll leave if you want. But I wanted to see if you are okay."

I shake my head. "I feel like I've been put in that paper bag with all those grimy memories, all that dirt, and then turned over, dropped on the hardwood floor with the pictures, letters and the dust of forty years. This is just crazy! Gut-wrenchingly nuts. I'll never know my real mother or my father."

I start bawling again, feel out of control.

Ron kneels down beside me and puts his hands on mine. I'm sitting on the commode and strands of hair are sticking to my face. I realized what I must look like and laugh.

"Are you laughing?"

"Yes, but I'm crying, too," I wail.

"We could try to find your biological father."

"What would be the point of that? I'm forty, and I don't care. I've gone this far without a father. He ran out on Charlotte." My feelings are way too personal to explain to someone I've only met a few weeks ago, but I have to let it out, and Ron is so understanding. "I always wondered why my mother didn't like me. Why my father stayed away. Now I know. Mystery over. That's all I need to know. My whole family was a big lie. You know, lies can really screw things up."

"They do."

"I've always lied to myself, about men, about what I want. Always. Maybe it runs in the family."

The honesty of my statement shakes me a little. I stand, go to the sink and turn on the cold water, wet a washcloth and hold it against my eyes. When I look in the mirror, I laugh at how bad I look. I brush my hair back, rub off the smeared mascara, then turn around.

"This is the real me. No distortions. I usually look like this. Scary as hell."

"You look fine."

"I thought we were talking about truth. What do you really want from me—sex? If that's all, I can give that to you. I've done that many times."

I press my lips together. Maybe that was a little too honest. Ron's got such a nice face, kind eyes.

"I want to be happy. That's all I'm looking for. I like you and I'm not an asshole. Why's that so hard to believe?" he asks.

"It just is. What do you want right now?"

"I'd like to get to know you better."

"It seems I let you know way too much about me already."

"How?"

"By…telling you all these things, and last night when I kissed you. I should not have done that."

"We're two adults—what's wrong with that? Let's not play games. So we kissed, big deal."

"I just want honesty, that's all."

"Then, your eyes are a little red."

"What?"

"You said something about the way you looked a minute ago. I said you looked fine. Honestly, your eyes are really red."

I laugh, sit down again, sigh. "All my life I've been handed a big pile of bullshit. From my mother, from myself, from husbands. Then I come back here and find out all this." My arms spread wide.

"All families have secrets. They aren't as big as your revelation, but no one knew why my dad never went back to college after he broke his leg. He ended up working for the city all his life in a low-level job."

"Maybe he couldn't afford to go back."

"If he couldn't afford college why didn't people say so?"

"Why don't you ask him?"

"Too late. He died four years ago."

"I'm sorry."

He leans against the wall, rubs his chin. "Actually I think he couldn't go back because he knocked my mother up with me. No one wanted to say that right to my face."

"It wasn't your fault."

"Yeah, I know," he says, and looks around. "You know, I've never had this long a conversation with someone in a bathroom."

"Let's go downstairs." We get up, walk back to the library in silence.

"I'm sorry about all that." I nod toward the ceiling. "I usually can hold it together a little better."

"You're always apologizing. Don't worry about it. You're human, that's all."

"Do you think I should read more letters?"

"No, not now. And I can go home if you need to rest."

I take a deep breath, feel tired from crying so hard. Yet it's nice having him in the house now.

"I'd like you to stay for a while," I say.

CHAPTER 19

Magnolia Hall
Greensville, NC
July 2000

I'm almost finished painting the new wall white—so white it looks icy. I got up early, showered and dressed, then I started, even before Tildy got here!

"Rise and shine, Miss Juliette. Rise and shine." Tildy's shoes squeak against the floor in between her words.

"I've risen, but I'm not shining."

She smiles as she walks into the bedroom, but when she sees the wall, she stops.

"What's wrong?" I ask.

"My lord, that wall without the magnolias looks mighty strange."

"The room looks brighter, newer."

"But it's always been wallpapered. I don't know if I like it."

"Paint is so much cheaper and easier to do." I try to talk her into liking it.

"You had breakfast yet?" she asks, ignoring what I've said.

I shake my head, put the roller in the tray.

"I'll get busy fixing you something." But before she leaves she looks around the room again. "I saw Charlotte's diary laying on the library floor. Did you read any of it?"

"No. I heated some leftovers for Ron, you know, to try and pay him back for putting up the wall."

"That's good." She looks at the bed then me. "Why you up so early?"

"I couldn't sleep."

"Why can't you sleep?" She glances at the unmade bed again.

"Don't get any ideas. We talked, read one letter. I *am* Charlotte's daughter," I say almost too matter-of-factly, and wish I wasn't so impetuous. "It said so in the letter I read. There's no doubt, even Ron thinks so. And the young man she was in love with, he's my father."

"That why you quit reading?" She wrinkles her nose. "We kinda knew that already."

I realize I'm pressing the roller against the wall so hard that my hand is beginning to hurt and shake.

"Yes. But I also found out that James—the man who I thought was my father—made up his mind not to see me because…" I stop, feel my throat tighten. I don't want to get any more upset than I am, but I need to explain to her. "Because he couldn't stand to look at me. I reminded him too much of Charlotte. Nice thing to find out about someone you thought was your father. And all this time I blamed my crazy mother for not letting me see him, for our shitty life. What a fool I was, am."

"Honey, you didn't know," she says, yet she looks down, as if she's ashamed for him. "I had heard tales your mama had wanted a baby. They adopted you."

I put the roller in the tray. "At least I know the truth— that he was selfish, self-absorbed and immature to start. He chose not to see me because he was chickenshit about Charlotte, putting it on my mother, blah, blah, blah." I wave my arms around. "Who cares? I don't."

"Honey, I know you must be hurt." She looks back at the wall. "What about Ron, what did he say?"

"Not much. I didn't give him time. I cried all over his shirt. Great way to avoid thinking about my problems."

"Oh," she says softly.

"This family never wanted anything to do with me, because my *real* father wasn't good enough. So it's going to stay that way. I don't want to know anything more about them."

Tildy looks so sad, and I feel like a shit for acting snotty. My life certainly isn't her fault.

I wipe my hands on the rag, walk over to her and touch her shoulder. "Why don't you take today off and read Charlotte's diary, some of the letters? You never have. You might enjoy it. And if you want you can keep them." Tildy should have the diary as partial payment for working here and keeping me company.

"I've got too much dusting to do. The new wall made such a mess. There's plaster dust all over the house, on the furniture. Besides, Mr. Grey told me what's in that diary."

"It doesn't matter if there's dust. And you should read the diary yourself." When she frowns, I add, "If I read the diary, will you keep it, read it? It's got nothing in there about me, I'm sure, so that's safe. And it's not even that long. I'm finished painting. We could read it together. Then it's yours. Will you do that for me?"

She looks at me and smiles. "If you read it, I will, too."

I'm sitting in the living room, staring out the window. Words from Charlotte's diary are squealing through my mind, forward and backward, a hundred miles an hour, reminding me that Tildy belongs to this family as much as I do. Grey never told her the truth—just fairy tales. And he left out the most important fact—he and Tildy are related.

Now it's up to me to tell her—there is no one else. My stomach tightens. Pots clang in the kitchen. It's almost five.

I stand, feel numb, a little sick to my stomach as I walk toward the kitchen. In the middle of the hall, I change my mind and head up the stairs. What in the world am I going to say to her? When I get to the bedroom, I take the plastic off the paint tray, pick up the roller and begin moving it back and forth.

Minutes later I hear Tildy enter the room. "What are you doing, honey? That wall is done. You said so yourself. Dinner's about ready."

I look at Tildy. She's standing in the middle of the room, and her face is gleaming with sweat, with hope. *Always hope.*

"You look worse than you did before," she says.

I don't know what to say. I look at the paint roller, put it down. "Who was Charity's husband?" I ask to get my bearings. Maybe she knows and has never said.

"Mr. Grey said she wasn't married."

"But who was the father of her child?"

"He said a field hand. Why all these questions?"

Anger toward Grey rises in me. If he was in front of me right now I'd slap him. "Tildy, I need to talk to you."

"'Bout what? You feeling bad again?"

I go to the bed, sit on the edge and pat the space beside me. She comes close yet doesn't sit down.

"I knew Grey didn't tell you."

"Tell me what? He told me a lot, honey."

I reach out, take her hand and hold it for a moment. She should know, and I'm angry that it's all up to me.

"Grey didn't tell you that you belong to this family."

She squints. "*Belong?* What do you mean?"

I have to just come out with it. "James Alexander and Charity had a baby together." I leave out the part of how he raped her—I can't say this to Tildy. "It's all in the diary."

She looks at me for a long moment, covers her lips then speaks through them. "Why, that just isn't true. Mr. Grey would have told me."

"It is. Why would Miss Charlotte lie? I guess Grey never could face the truth about that, either."

"Mr. Grey would have told me something like that, I know he would have."

"Why would Miss Charlotte write it? Do you know what a horrible thing that was in those days, what a chance she took writing it down? I guess she wanted us to know." My forehead throbs with hurt for Tildy.

"It's in her diary?" Her eyes are wide with disbelief.

"Come on." I take her hand again and guide her out of the room, down the stairs. A moment later I open the diary to the page where Charlotte wrote about her husband and Charity, want to tell her to read it, but I can't. It all seems so raw.

Tildy takes the book from me, scans the page then stares straight ahead, her lips pursed.

"I am so sorry, so sorry. You belong to this family. And he never told you, never hinted."

"He didn't but maybe he didn't realize—"

"Tildy, he did. He had to, as much as he loved the house, the history. Be honest with yourself. He didn't want you to know," I say softly, feeling such a bond with her, because of what we've both found out. "Maybe it was too hard for him to talk about the situation. He might have been ashamed, but it's true, you're an Alexander."

I leave out the thoughts that plague me—he hid the diary for a reason. He didn't expect anybody to find those pictures, the letters, any of it till the house was torn down. He didn't want anyone to know, but he should have at least told Tildy before he died.

Tildy sits, presses back on the couch, the diary still open on her lap. She closes her eyes. I sit down next to her and take her hand. Her skin feels so soft, warm. She pulls away, crosses her arms, looks down at the yellowing page, then closes it and stands.

"I've got things to do in the kitchen."

"Tildy, please, wait! The other day I didn't tell you this, but I was thinking how nice it would be if you were my mom. You're not, but at least now we know we're related."

Without a smile, a word, she walks out of the room. I run down the hall, find her in the kitchen. She looks at me. "You want something?"

"Do you need to talk? We need to talk."

"I've got work to do. We can talk later."

"Tildy, I am so sorry he never told you. What you said about how I released Charlotte from the wall, don't you think I released you, too, maybe even me? I feel so different now. You're part of this family, we—" I stop.

"Oh, honey, I know." Tildy wraps me in her arms and we pat each other.

"You've been so nice to me. I'm sorry about this," I say. We break away, sit at the table. "He should have told you, and he should have told me," I say again.

"Maybe he couldn't stand the pain of everything," Tildy says.

"It was such a cowardly thing to do, to not tell, and then hide everything. He didn't care about you, he didn't care about me, all he must have cared about was the family's honor."

The quizzical expression drains from her face.

"He should have told you or let you read the diary. He knew he was dying. He could have contacted me and told me the truth about my parents, told you, left you the house, for God's sake."

"Now, I know and you know," she says softly. "Maybe it's better this way, that I found out from you. Brings us closer. Don't you see? I loved young Miss Charlotte and now I've found you." She gets up, faces the sink and turns on the water full blast.

The way her voice cracked tells me this is true. And thank God I'm smart enough to leave her alone.

Tildy left tonight without saying goodbye and her silence told me a lot about how she's feeling. Maybe like me—numb, overwhelmed and stunned. I've been so worried about getting the money from the house I never even thought to ask where she goes every night.

I walk into the living room. Tildy left Charlotte's diary open, pressed against the couch, the spine of the book bent. I close it and go to the library. The pictures are still scattered on the floor. I sit next to them and pick one up.

Charlotte standing on the porch.

My biological mother. The thought seems so strange. I wonder what she was like, and what kind of mother she would have been. She was so young. I stare at her image, her belly and wonder if she was pregnant with me. My chest aches, and I turn the picture over, look for a date but there isn't any. I place it with the others.

Another picture. The person who I thought was my father smiling, standing out in the carport, shadows thrown across his young face. He's just another person I never really knew, will never know. Grey is standing next to him, his arms hanging by his sides.

I stir the pictures, find one at the bottom, pull it out. Tildy. So young! Her face is thinner, more angular, and she's smiling. There's a little of Alex there. I try to see if she looks like any of the Alexanders but can't see a resemblance. She's standing in the far corner of the yard by the biggest magnolia, looking as if she's waiting for something spectacular. I wonder if the picture was taken before or after she met Johnny.

The doorbell rings, jolts me.

Ron smiles when I open the front door. Oh, God.

"Hi," he says before I do.

I brush my hair back. "Hi. Come in." We stand in the hallway, the sunlight rushing through the sidelights, making everything bright.

"I came to help paint," Ron says, points to the upstairs.

"Too late, it's done. I did it all this morning."

He looks at his watch then back. "You must have gotten up early."

"I did. I couldn't sleep. I read Charlotte's diary this morning." We walk into the living room. "I got to the part in the diary where my relative rapes Tildy's great-great-grandmother and I stopped."

Ron studies me. "You aren't kidding, are you?" When I don't say anything, he clears his throat. "I guess that's something you don't joke about."

"No, and to top it all off, Charity, Tildy's great-great-grandmother, had a baby from that rape. Tildy and I are related and Grey Alexander, the prick that he *was*, never told her. If I hadn't found the diary…" I pick it up, put it down, and realize I still have Tildy's picture in my hand. I place it inside the book. "If I hadn't knocked down that mildewed wall, we never would have found out. Can you imagine Tildy never finding that out? How unfair."

"I'm not surprised. Some of the older folks never wanted to admit the terrible things that happened back then."

I sit beside him. "She went home without saying goodbye for the first time since I've been here."

For a few moments neither of us says anything.

"How could he let her work here, let her spend her money? Let her be his servant without telling her. He must have known how much she loved the house. How she's so devoted to it."

"Is she coming back?"

A deep hurt pulses through me. "Do you think she won't come back? I have no idea where she lives."

"That's easy to find out. But I think she'll come back."

"Good, because I'm going to give her Magnolia Hall." I

say the words before I think about what I'm saying, yet when they're out I'm glad.

"You have no legal responsibility to give her any part of your inheritance, the money. None at all."

"That's lawyer talk. The money that was going to fix my life? Money's not going to do that."

Ron pats my shoulder.

"So you don't think I should give her the house?" I ask, testing him, wanting him to say the wrong thing, so I can leave without any attachments.

"I was just advising you as your lawyer. Personally, I think you should do what you want to—what feels right to you."

"What would you do?"

"I'd give her the house."

"Can you draw up the papers?"

"Sure, simple form. But you should ask her before you do anything."

"Yeah, I guess I have to ask her, of course, but she's getting the house. I don't have to think anymore." And for the first time in my life I feel free, know I'm doing something right.

"You thinking of staying?" Ron asks.

"I can't. Really. My life was pretty crappy. I just got divorced, just got fired. I've probably been thrown out of my apartment by now."

"That's easy to fix. You'll get your life straightened out."

"I hope so. But I have to find that out before I stay here. I have to go back, think, get what possessions I have, then maybe I'll come back in a few weeks, or a few months."

"Good," he says.

"If you don't mind, will you get the papers ready for Tildy tomorrow?"

After Ron left this evening, I crawled into bed. I left the old drapes open and the newly painted wall is filled with large squares of moonlight. The silver is so much better than the faded flowers. I wonder if my mother, Charlotte, gazed at the moonlight against the wall. How alone and hopeless she must have felt. Would she be happy knowing I was here, that I found out about her? I guess I have to be satisfied not ever knowing.

"You want to give me the house?" Tildy says as I sit in the kitchen chair next to hers.

I nod, smile. I slept well, and this morning I feel better than I have since I met Bill.

"Tildy, if you don't have bad feelings about the place, it should be yours. Ron drew up the papers. All we have to do is sign them." I look at her, love her face, her expression.

"You're my family. As you told me, a gift is a gift and you can't give it back."

I tap the papers Ron brought by a few minutes ago. He and I hugged, and he told me he'd drive me to the airport. That's when I realized I don't have any money to fly home.

"Lord have mercy," Tildy whispers. "I still love this place despite all I found out. The memories are still here, the strength. I still can't desert my people—" she looks at me "—our people."

"Does that mean yes? Are you okay? I was worried about you yesterday. I'm sorry you found out what you did, but now we're family. I'm Charlotte's daughter. Those words sound so strange. Do you think I'll ever get used to them?"

Tildy studies the papers then me, and shakes her head. "You're part of my family. It took me some time yesterday, but I guess I knew it and just didn't want to believe it. Mr. Grey, he sometimes, well, when he had a drink or two, would look at me funny, shake his head." She sighs, stares at her hands for a long moment. "I wasn't being honest with myself."

"I know the feeling," I say.

"Honey, we always had a connection. Whether it was blood or something else. You were just too busy trying to get out of here to realize it."

I laugh. "I know."

"So you want me to take the house, have it be mine?"

"Yes, I'm going back to Vegas, to straighten out my life, but I'll try to help you."

"Are you coming back? What about your fella?"

"Tildy, he's not my boyfriend. We hardly know each other. I have to go back. I promise I'll come home." The last word slips out before I can stop it. *Home*. Maybe one day it will be.

"See, I knew you'd come around my way. This is your home. And I want to make it that way for you and Alexandria."

"So you'll take the house? You'll live here."

"If you want to give it to me, then I will. I don't want to be rude. But, honey, let me give you a little money."

I breathe in, realize I need the money for a plane ticket. And suddenly love wells in my heart for this woman.

"Okay, if you're sure you have enough."

She nods. "Course I have enough. My land, you're giving me a house. The wall's fixed. Wouldn't Miss Charlotte, your mama, just lose it if she knew? She'd be so happy." She leans back, looks around the kitchen like she has never seen it before. "My, my." She stands. "You know what I always wanted to do?"

I look up and smile. Her sunny outlook is infectious. "What have you always wanted to do?"

"I always thought Magnolia Hall could be a wonderful bed-and-breakfast. I mentioned it to Mr. Grey when he was having so much financial trouble, and he just shook his head. He didn't want to share with no one, you know. I think people would like to know about the house, don't you think? The history. Why, I could tell them about my memories, show them things, tell them about my ancestors. I'd do breakfast, maybe dinner, too. People seem to like my cooking, and I could see to it they ate well before they went on their ways. You and I could do it together. You could be in charge of the repairs, then you wouldn't have to deal cards no more."

I stand, throw my arms around her, hug her hard. She laughs and so do I. "I think it's a wonderful idea, if that's what you want to do."

"Why, I might just do that, and when you come back you could help me. But right now, I want to go look at the wall, enjoy what you did, then I'll run down to the bank and get you some money. Then I'll cook. You know you should ask that nice young man over to dinner before you leave. And then I want to make sure the carpets are clean so when I go get some antiques, they'll be ready. By then, you might be back."

I look at her, smile and throw my arms around her. "Welcome home, Tildy Butler."

HARLEQUIN® Next™

Coming this September

In the first of Charlotte Douglas's Maggie Skerritt mysteries, an experienced police detective has to predict a serial killer's next move while charting her course for the future. But will Maggie's longtime friend and confidant add another life-altering event to the mix?

PELICAN BAY
Charlotte Douglas

www.TheNextNovel.com

Four new novels available every month, wherever Harlequin books are sold.

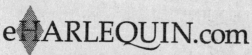

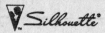